Fleeing the Sharks

A Cuban Family Story

Linda Hardister Rodriguez

LYSTRA BOOKS
& Literary Services

Fleeing the Sharks: A Cuban Family Story
© 2016 by Linda Hardister Rodriguez
All rights reserved.
ISBN 978-0-9911502-8-1 printed book
ISBN 978-0-9911502-9-8 ebook

Library of Congress Control Number 2016937075
Fiction — General

Summary: A prominent Cuban family at first welcomes the success of the Castro revolution, hoping to see the new government end corruption and bring prosperity and democracy to the poor of their beloved island. Gradually they realize that their dreams were just that, and the new reality is harsh. The story is told through the eyes of their teenaged son who watches as his extended family becomes disillusioned and eventually is forced to flee.

This is a work of fiction that loosely represents actual experiences of the author's husband and his family. Some characters, incidents, and dialogue come from the writer's imagination.

Book design by Kelly Prelipp Lojk

LYSTRA BOOKS
& Literary Services

Published by Lystra Books & Literary Services, LLC
391 Lystra Estates Drive, Chapel Hill, NC 27517
919-968-7877 | lystrabooks@gmail.com

—————————cᴧᴐ—————————

To my husband and his Cuban family

—————————ᴣᴡᴒ—————————

AUTHOR'S NOTE: *This story is based on true events
that occurred in my husband's life and in Cuba between
January 1, 1959, and September 15, 1960. He appears
with his mother at his high school graduation in the photo
on the back of the book. The woman in the photo beside
them is his beloved godmother.*

FLORIDA
Atlantic Ocean
Gulf of Mexico
HAVANA
CUBA
Matanzas
Santa Clara
Cienfuegos
Bay of
Pigs
Camaguey
Caribbean Sea

August 14, 2015

*F*rancisco stopped pedaling his stationary bike as the TV news announcer said, "In two minutes, you will witness United States history taking a sharp turn left." Pointing to the ten-foot-high glass doors of the United States Embassy in Havana, he added, "Secretary of State John Kerry will exit the embassy to preside over the raising of an American flag in Cuba for the first time since that flag was lowered, returned to Washington, and retired fifty-four years, seven months, and eleven days ago."

My God, Francisco thought, I was standing outside those embassy doors exactly fifty-five years ago — mid-August 1960 — waiting to get my visa. I thought the United States would put an end to the chaos in Cuba and stop Fidel and his communists. At sixteen I believed I was going to the U.S. for a year, just long enough to learn English.

He remembered the day he heard President Eisenhower had broken diplomatic relations with Cuba — January 3, 1961. It had been one day after all but eleven U.S.

diplomats had been accused of spying and expelled from the country.

His brother, José, had called him in Louisiana. "Stop thinking of home," he told Francisco. "We're here for the long haul."

The TV camera shifted from the embassy courtyard to a view of the bay and then to Havana's shoreline. The announcer said, "This beautiful island is known as the 'Pearl of the Antilles'."

When a picture of the courtyard reappeared, the announcer continued with his description of Cuba. He said that while her shape was similar to a crocodile, she instead had the grace, intelligence, and playfulness of a slender bottlenose dolphin diving into the warm Caribbean Sea. With the churning Atlantic at her back, the lovely creature pushed her nose southward and rested her tail in the placid waters of the Gulf of Mexico. Her body extended seven hundred forty-seven miles from east to west and her narrow waist was but twenty miles north to south.

The announcer looked down at his desk and read from the material in front of him. He described tiny low islands lying off her back and chest, filled with three hundred species of birds, including macaws, hummingbirds, and parakeets. He talked of mountains that grew mahogany, ebony, rosewood, cedar, and pine forests and said that thirty types of palm trees dotted her soil. She was surrounded by wahoo, shark, barracuda — more than nine hundred kinds of fish — which swam in waters with an average temperature of seventy-seven degrees. Violent hurricanes out of Africa lashed her in fall while northeasterly trade winds and refreshing rains soothed her in summer.

"Ah, truly, this beautiful land is a paradise," the announcer faced the camera again. "But forgive me. I digress. We have business to attend to."

Francisco gripped the bike's handlebars with sweaty hands, then swiped at the gray hair wet on his neck. "Of course it's beautiful. But those sons of bitches stole it and then ruined it."

The camera pointed to a row of 1950s-era American cars painted yellow, red, and royal blue parked along a seaside boulevard — the Malecón — before it focused on a nearby six-story building. There large U.S. and Cuban flags hung side by side from a balcony. Same colors, Francisco thought, except the Cuban one has blue and white stripes with a single white star in the center of a red triangle. The camera returned to the cars. One looked like a 1954 Chrysler. Could that be his mother's?

Francisco leapt from the bike and stood closer to the TV. He spoke directly to the screen: "You criminals! You throw Cubans in prison for speaking their minds. You take the money tourists bring, then live like kings and pay the military and secret police while your own people go hungry. You disgust me! Your flag may have the same colors as ours but your government is nothing like America's!"

The camera faced the front courtyard of the embassy. The three retired Marines, now with gray hair, who had lowered the flag in 1961 handed a new one to three young Marines in blue dress uniforms. While the younger men gently unfolded the new flag beside a massive steel flagpole, a drum roll began. The beat started slowly, then picked up speed, before giving way to a brass band playing "The Star-Spangled Banner" as the red, white, and blue flag soared to the sky. Loud cheers arose from the guests inside the twelve-foot wrought-iron fence and others who had gathered outside on the sidewalk.

Secretary of State Kerry, his chin lifted, stood erect at a wooden lectern. Wearing a pale blue tie the color of the cloudless sky and the peaceful waters of the Straits of Florida behind him, he said, "It's time to unfurl our flags, raise them up, and let the world know that we wish each other well."

"Don't believe what they say. They're liars! Masters of destruction!" Francisco shouted at the television, as tears welled up. "How can we be giving in to those murderers?" he whispered.

"Our leaders — President Obama and President Castro — made a courageous decision to stop being prisoners of history," Kerry continued, seeming to answer Francisco's question.

But it was all chaff blown to the wind to Francisco. What about the people who became real prisoners because they wouldn't join the Communist Party? he asked himself. And what about my mother and father? Forever buried in a foreign land instead of lying beside their parents in Havana.

"We remain convinced that the people of Cuba would be best served by genuine democracy," Kerry said, "where people are free to choose their leaders, express their ideas, and practice their faith..."

"Yes! That's the point." Francisco howled at the screen. "We had our troubles, but now you're shaking hands with those communist bastards who threw a net over that beautiful land and stomped on her." He lifted the bottom of his T-shirt and wiped the tears from his face.

December 31, 1958

*T*ío — Uncle — Eduardo held his crystal champagne glass high when he turned to face his wife and her family. His eyes twinkled in the candlelight. "This will truly be a new..." Pop! Pop! Pop!

Fireworks, Francisco thought. Or gunfire.

Eduardo set his glass of Veuve Clicquot on the table, shouting, "Just a minute!" as he dashed to the balcony.

Francisco leapt from the living room couch to follow his uncle, when he heard his mother call, "Stop! Come back in here, you two! Might be gunfire."

"But it could be fireworks, Mami," Francisco yelled as he leaned over the wrought-iron railing. Then he muttered, "And I could have watched some if you had let me go to Roberto's party."

Eduardo placed his arm around his nephew's shoulder. "Now, now. Your mother is correct. We shouldn't be out here. Maybe a stray bullet or two, who knows?"

"Who do you think is winning, revolutionaries or secret

6

police?" Francisco asked. "Can a bullet reach to the third floor?"

Eduardo led his nephew back inside and picked up his glass, holding it even higher, to continue his toast. "Change is coming. To a democratic Cuba!"

Francisco's mother, father, sister, and three aunts nodded, said, "Umm," raised their glasses, and drank.

"Dios — God — I hope you're right," his father said. He sighed and shook his head. "We need an end to this turmoil. It's been going on much too long."

"Yeah, my whole life," Francisco said.

Francisco's father, Pedro, motioned for his son to sit down on the floor beside his chair. "That's true. You were born in '44 and Batista organized his first rebellion against the government in 1933."

Francisco looked up at his father. "Guess I forgot about the first time. I was thinking of his coup d'état in 1952."

Pedro nodded. "Just before June elections, the bastard — pardon me, ladies — shredded our constitution, set up his dictatorship, and began enriching himself and his friends with kickbacks from public works projects, U.S. corporate investments, and those casino mobsters."

"And now, our savior comes along," Eduardo said.

"You're more confident than I am, but you're the genius of the family. I only hope you're right," said Pedro.

"But Papy, most people are supporting Fidel," Francisco said.

"Well, Batista was stupid," Pedro said, adding that Batista had created a brutal secret police force that terrorized and murdered anyone who threatened him. "So people

7

turned to Fidel and his promise of democracy. We'll see what the future holds."

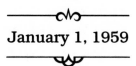

January 1, 1959

*F*rancisco's white shutters glowed in a pattern of horizontal stripes when he awoke. The clock radio on his bedside table showed 9:20. He had slept seven hours. He stumbled around his brother Ramón's empty bed, pushed the shutters aside, and scanned Calzada Street two stories below. Then he looked to his right toward the Gulf of Mexico. Large cumulus clouds drifted across the azure sky and royal palms swayed in the light breeze between Malecón Boulevard and the shore.

He opened his bedroom door and saw that someone had laid a newspaper on the cream-colored granite floor.

"Batista Flees!" shouted the top half of the front page. The lower portion read: "Señoras y Señores — Ladies and Gentlemen — our beloved island is free." Page Two told of higher-level military and government employees confiscating yachts or flying out on military and commercial planes to escape to Florida or The Bahamas with their families.

Noticing he was still wearing his pants and shirt from the

night before, Francisco smoothed his shirt as he ran down the hallway and into the living room where his older sister, Luisa, lay on the couch, a book propped on her chest so she could see it and the TV.

"President Fulgencio Batista fled to the Dominican Republic with his family and friends at three this morning, taking a very large sum of money with him. And," the announcer said, "Fidel's men are coming. The Twenty-sixth of July Movement are on their way down the central highway. Coming here! To us!" The background music, "Mamá, son de las lomas" — Mama, they're from the hills — was a song Francisco had only heard whispered about, because it was banned from all stations except the illegal Rebel Radio.

The announcer continued: "People are on a rampage. Casinos are being looted and slot machines dragged into the street with tables and chairs, everything. They're burning them. They're smashing the parking meters that Batista's brother-in-law installed to rob us. Mobs are stealing from Batista's cronies' houses, the ones who left with him this morning. The American Embassy told tourists to stay in their hotels, but they've swamped the airport, trying to get off the island."

Luisa pointed a slender finger at her younger brother. "Mami said, 'Do not leave this house.' She and Papy are with Tía — Aunt — Julia and Tío Eduardo."

Francisco slumped to the floor in front of the television and remained there for hours, not wanting to miss any of the reporter's words, not even to go to the kitchen for food. The news didn't stop. "The airport has been closed. People are dancing in the street. Music is everywhere. Police are aiming their guns at rioters but not shooting." He added that American actor George Raft was standing atop a gaming table pleading with people not to destroy the Capri — the casino he ran with the mobster Trafficante. He asked them to sit down and let him bring food from the kitchen.

January 2, 1959

*T*he television reporter grinned so widely that he was hardly able to talk. "Look," he observed. "Che Guevara is in Havana and is taking charge."

The screen switched to a photo of a young man with a bright, open face. A face like a woman's, Francisco thought. His curly hair brushed the shoulders of his olive-green military fatigues. A black beret, a small red star pinned to the front, hugged his head. He stood, holding a cigar, in front of the Fortaleza de la Cabaña — the colonial fortress the Spaniards had completed in 1774 and used as a prison.

"He's taken charge of Havana. His headquarters is there. In the prison!"

January 4, 1959

$\mathcal{F}$rancisco yawned as he dipped his toast into his café con leche — coffee with milk. The excitement of Batista's departure and wondering when Fidel would arrive in Havana had made for a restless night.

Pedro joined the family at the breakfast table and announced, "We're going to Abuela de Veinte y uno's — Grandmother from Twenty-one's — house today for lunch. Same as any Sunday." He glanced at Silvia when she sighed. "Mami's concerned about our safety, but my mother will be worried if we don't come, and I don't want to upset her. I had promised to bring her huesitos de santos — bones of saints — pastries, but we won't go out as far as La Casa Suárez Bakery. We'll just pick up something else nearby, and leave at 12:30."

Francisco loved the huesitos de santos marzipan shaped like small, soft bone, white on the outside and yellow inside, as much as his abuela did. His mouth watered. Next Sunday, he thought. By then things will settle down and we can go to La Casa Suárez.

Both of Francisco's grandmothers were named María. To distinguish them, his father's mother was referred to as Abuela de Twenty-one because she lived on Twenty-first Street with her sister Sofia and her two unmarried daughters, Clara and Regina. Francisco's family had lunch with the four women every Sunday, then sat on the front porch and talked until Pedro left for the racetrack and the young people went to a movie or a ball-game with friends.

Francisco's mother drove slowly, swiveling her head from one sidewalk to the other and stepping on the brake once or twice before reaching each stoplight along the twenty blocks.

"Silvia," her husband said, "You're making this dangerous. Relax and drive."

"You know I'm just being cautious, Pedro, because I don't think we should be here."

Francisco was puzzled. "But I thought it was over, Mami. Why are you so worried?"

"Hijo — son," Silvia replied, "don't you still hear shots at night? Who knows what trouble we might face around the next corner."

When they arrived at the two-story shotgun house that Francisco's grandmother rented, she was waiting on the porch in her wheelchair. Six years earlier, she had broken her hip and had refused to have it pinned, even though her son, Francisco's father, was an orthopedic surgeon.

For the fourth time since they had sat for their lunch of arroz con pollo, Abuela begged her son, "Please don't go to work tomorrow." She pushed the chicken, red bell peppers, rice, and peas around her plate with her fork, refusing

14

to eat even when encouraged. "It's much too dangerous. No patients will be there. Why do you want to worry your mother?"

Pedro propped his knife and fork on the edge of his plate and faced his mother. "Mamá, I'll be in the operating room and in my office Monday morning just as I have since 1948 when I opened the Orthopedic Hospital. It's my duty." He patted her hand. "It's OK. There haven't been gunshots during the day since Che took over. The pharmacy can do without Silvia for another week. She'll keep Francisco and Luisa at home until Dia de los Reyes is over and they're back in school."

January 6, 1959

*"C*ome on, you lazy slug." Luisa pounded on Francisco's door. "Mami wants to open presents. Papy has to go to the hospital to check on something. Now, get up!"

It was the Day of the Three Kings. Francisco leapt out of bed. He reached into a drawer, pulled on a T-shirt and pants, and wondered when he had ever had to be dragged out of bed to open gifts.

His mother sat in the living room in her favorite chair — the mahogany and cane rocker — beside the Christmas tree. Francisco was surprised to see her with unbrushed hair and wearing the same clothes as the day before. Rosa, their cook, came in from the kitchen carrying a tray of café con leche and slices of the chocolate cake Tía Clara had sent home with them two days before. Silvia tapped her foot on the hard granite floor and sighed. "We're taking the tree down right after you open presents. We have to do something. I'm tired of waiting for our lives to start again."

January 8, 1959

Although Francisco felt more exhausted with each passing day, he slept with his shutters open so the light would awaken him in case something happened and his alarm didn't go off. He lurched past Ramón's bed and leaned out the window, shivering in the cool breeze from the Gulf. More people than usual were on the street. Was that a good sign or not?

Too bad Batista had been so afraid student revolutionaries would organize against him at Havana University that he closed it, Francisco thought. Then he chuckled. But looked like he needed to have been worried. If the university hadn't closed, José wouldn't be studying medicine, and Ramón architecture, at Tulane University in New Orleans. They'd be right here at the University of Havana trying to tell me what to do and what to think like always. Having brothers three and seven years older is tough most of the time, but now when I could use their advice about this new revolution, they're not here.

On his way to the kitchen, Francisco saw *Diario de la Marina* — *La Marina* — the largest daily newspaper in Havana, on the dining table. It had been folded so that only the top article on the front page could be seen. "The administration of U.S. President Dwight D. Eisenhower recognizes the new government of Cuba. He appoints a new ambassador to replace Earl T. Smith, the friend of Batista. The criminal Batista and his cronies took three hundred million dollars with them when they fled."

Francisco stopped reading when he heard a voice behind the kitchen door. "Today — it's today!" the radio announcer said. "People are joining him all along the route. Hundreds. Maybe thousands! Coming to Havana today." He paused. The Cuban National anthem played in the background. "Up Twenty-third Street. Starting at the ocean on the Malecón to Columbus Cemetery. All of them. A parade!"

He opened the door and saw his mother perched on the edge of a wooden chair at the small square table in the corner of the room, her head turned to the side with one ear six inches in front of the radio. Her face glowed.

Rosa wore a grin when she turned to Francisco. "Café con leche, Panchito?"

"Mami, is he really here? Where can we see him? And when?" Now I don't need Ramón and José, he thought. It's done. Over. He's here and everything will be all right.

Francisco's mother rose and grasped his hand. "Hijo, we'll see him. See them all! Your father will come when he can. Go. Knock on your sister's door and tell her to get dressed. I have to get my hat." She motioned to Rosa. "Put the coffee down. Go to your room and get dressed. Come on, everyone, let's go!"

As his mother was locking the outside door behind them, Francisco realized he had forgotten to brush his hair, so he ran his fingers through the thick, brown mass.

The four of them — Francisco and Luisa out front, his mother and Rosa behind — passed anyone walking slower, along the packed sidewalks of K Street. Men, women, and children — shouting and laughing — all moved in the same direction. By the time they reached Twenty-third Street, the women were panting. Silvia pulled on the back of Francisco's jacket and said, "Stay together," pointing to the right. Then she pushed Rosa in behind Luisa and Francisco.

When they reached the corner of Avenida de Los Presidentes, Silvia pointed to a doorway. Francisco noticed beads of sweat standing on her forehead. He looked at Rosa. Her face was bright red.

"Graciela lives in the apartment on top. We'll watch from her balcony." Silvia nodded her head.

Graciela greeted her friend with a hug and led them through open French doors onto a three-by-six-foot patio where her two young daughters stood on tiptoe on the base of a thick cement balustrade leaning over as far as they could. Francisco looked down at the street, then at the balconies and windows all around them. So much music poured from open windows that he couldn't separate the songs enough to identify them. People streamed in and out of doorways with their arms raised, snapping their fingers, and shaking their hips in rhythm to whatever music they heard.

Many women were dressed with hats and high heels as if they were going to work or mass. Men wore stiffly starched white guayabera shirts or short-sleeved shirts. A number of them looked as if they had just arrived from the countryside, dressed as they were in worn denim shirts and loose pants. Francisco watched an old man — his face brown and creased — at an open window across Twenty-third Street. He wore a straw hat tilted to one side, and a shirt buttoned partway up, exposing gray chest-hair. Half a cigar was clamped between his teeth, the corners of his mouth turned up as if he was trying to smile without losing it. Francisco caught his eye and raised both fists above his head. The older man gave him a thumbs-up.

Francisco lifted his chin and sniffed. The scent of coffee filled the air. Vendors' carts on street and sidewalks were surrounded by people waving pesos and shouting orders for churros, ice cream, and blue shaved ice. Cuban flags flew from balconies and windows. Look at this celebration, he thought. How excited they are. This is what we need — freedom. Now we can go out at night without being afraid we'll be picked up by the secret police. He shivered when he remembered the night a friend's father — a judge — was driving his son and Francisco to a party. They were stopped by men with machine guns and forced to get out of the car and explain where they were going. If they hadn't had the card Batista's son had given his classmates that identified them as his friends, he wondered what would have happened. He shivered again. Now the police will have to follow the law, he thought. No more having to know someone to be safe from that big fat police chief, Rafael Salas Canizares.

More shouts. "Here they come. Look. There they are!" Francisco turned to his left toward the bay and saw a tank moving slowly under the Firestone, Esso, and Hotel San Carlos signs. Men in olive-green fatigues hung from its sides and crowded on top of it.

"We made it!" they yelled to the cheering people they passed.

One fighter in front spread his arms as if embracing the people. Another pumped a fist above his head. A woman ran into the street and lay down in front of a yellow 1957 Chevrolet traveling beside the tank. Two young men jumped off the tank, picked her up, and gently laid her on the sidewalk. Francisco saw her lying there, eyes closed with a peaceful look on her face. Maybe she's so happy, she just can't figure out how to express it, he thought.

Then Francisco saw him, the man they all were waiting for. He grasped his mother's shoulder and shouted, "Mami, he's here. It's over!" Yes, I'm free now, he thought.

The people on the balcony turned in the direction of Francisco's outstretched arm and witnessed their miracle-worker. Fidel Alejandro Castro Ruz. A twenty-six-year-old law graduate of Havana University and the son of a wealthy farmer, he sat in the bed of an open truck leaning on another man's shoulder. He wore olive-green fatigues and pill-box cap with a small brim. His beard and mustache were thick and curly.

Young soldiers wearing rosaries on the outside of their shirts rode on the hood and running boards of Fidel's truck and more walked alongside carrying rifles. Francisco had heard from his Christian Brother teachers that many of

21

the young fighters worshipped the Virgen Caridad del Cobre — the patron saint of Cuba who had appeared before three sailors in a storm and saved them from drowning. And, since Fidel had made military uniforms and facial hair requirements for these revolutionaries from the Sierra Maestra Mountains, they wore beards — hence the nickname barbudos.

A dozen or so field workers wearing muslin shirts, wide leather belts, and straw hats with small Cuban flags pinned to the front followed the truck on horseback — their long cattle ropes looped around their saddle horns.

When Fidel's truck halted at the corner nearest Graciela's building, Francisco bolted from the apartment, raced down the stairs, and crawled under the moving crowd to get to the front. Other Fidel well-wishers stepped on his hands and one kicked him in the side, but he was determined to get close to his hero. When he surfaced beside the truck, Fidel saw him, grinned, and saluted him. Wow, Francisco thought. Wait until I tell the guys. I've just been saluted by the most famous man in Cuba.

Fidel towered over the men beside him. Francisco thought he looked uncertain — maybe even frightened. Once he started talking, his facial expression hardened. "Democracia. Libertad." He raised his clenched left fist above his head and slammed it on the metal frame of the truck windshield. "No more dictators! Gracias a Dios — Thank God. Elections in eighteen months. Democracy. Gracias a Dios."

While Fidel elaborated on these ideas, a white dove released to celebrate his arrival landed on his left shoulder.

Another landed upon his open right hand. When he moved his head to look at the one on his shoulder, it remained still. He turned back to the people and continued his reassurances. The crowd roared. Three nuns standing beside Francisco dropped to their knees and crossed themselves, crying, "Gracias a Dios."

People shouted "Fidel, Fidel!" and climbed on the tires of the truck, reaching for him. A man wearing a white hat with a rolled-up brim jerked the new leader's hand so hard that he lost his balance and fell against a soldier holding an M-3 submachine gun. Men and women grabbed at his legs. Several soldiers jumped down to the street and eased the crowd back as the truck rolled forward.

When Francisco returned to Graciela's apartment, his mother wrapped an arm around his waist. "This is all for you, my hijo. A mother's wish come true! You will be fifteen years old in twenty-four days." She stretched out her arms toward the procession below. "Now, you have a future where you can choose your life and be safe."

In the evening newspaper, Francisco discovered that a great number of people interpreted the doves' landing on Fidel's shoulder and hand as a sign that the African god, Obatalá, had chosen him to lead the nation. While he hadn't heard of that particular god, he knew that the Santería — Way of the Saints — religion in Cuba was a combination of the beliefs and practices of Yoruban people brought to Cuba as slaves from west Nigeria and those of Roman Catholicism. Santería worshipers revered Roman Catholic saints and the Virgin Mary, though their practices involved black magic, animal sacrifice, voodoo, and mediums reaching deep into the spirit world through self-motivated trances. They believed doves were messengers from the god of purity.

January 12, 1959

*F*rancisco waited with Luisa on the sidewalk in front of their apartment building while his mother backed their car out of the driveway. They were going back to school. He leaned over and smoothed down his khaki pants. He had been especially careful when getting dressed to make sure his uniform wasn't wrinkled or stained. He gave another tug to the knot of his tie. It was important that this day be perfect. When his mother lined up the car by the curb and stopped, he slid into the back seat. The small bus from Luisa's school, The Sacred Heart Academy, stopped at the corner. She waved goodbye and ran toward it.

Silvia gently pounded the car horn with her fist, not enough to make a sound that her husband could hear but enough — Francisco thought — to express her frustration. The two of them stared at the wrought-iron and glass door at the bottom of the stairway that led to their third-floor apartment.

"What could your father be doing?" she blurted out. "You'll be late for school, and I need to get to work. I haven't set foot in that pharmacy for two weeks. Who knows what's happened?"

When Silvia stopped the car in front of his school, Colegio De la Salle, Francisco jumped out without saying goodbye, ran past the open wrought-iron gate, and stopped beside the marble statue of Saint John the Baptist in the front courtyard. He looked up at the three-story stone building that filled an entire city block and searched for the words carved in stone over the entrance, Dios, Patria, and Hogar: God, Fatherland, and Home. Tears came to his eyes. How relieved he was to have life back to normal.

Colegio De la Salle was a boys' school, grades one through twelve, owned and operated by the Christian Brothers Order of the Roman Catholic Church. Francisco was proud to go to this well-respected school and knew when the time came, he would be prepared for college.

The wide, dark hallway was filled with high-school boys dressed like Francisco — in uniforms of light blue shirts with large collars, dark blue ties, and khaki pants. When he reached his classroom, Brother Alfonso was standing solemnly behind his desk. Francisco's thirty-five classmates stood erect and quiet beside their desks. Francisco chuckled. Brother Alfonso looked like his nickname, Remache: short nail. A strict disciplinarian and tough as nails, rumor had it he had served in the French Foreign Legion before becoming a Christian Brother. He was feared and loved.

Remache waited until the last of his pupils arrived before beginning.

"Listen carefully," he said. "You must remember this. Now that our country has been liberated from a hideous dictator, God is giving you the greatest opportunity of your lives — to build a truly equal and just society. Rarely does a nation have the opportunity to dramatically improve itself. We have the foundation already in place with our large middle class, eight-hour work-day, minimum wage for cane cutters, and pensions for the elderly."

He continued by reminding his students that Cuba had a literacy rate of seventy-six percent. In the Western Hemisphere the country was third in life expectancy, first in per capita ownership of televisions, second in car ownership, and fifth in income. Cuba already had the second-highest standard of living in Latin America.

"But we won't reach the standards of our northern friends until the bottom twenty-five percent of our countrymen have electricity and running water. When their children attend school and have good health care you can be proud of your country! You are its future leaders — our teachers, doctors, lawyers, engineers, scientists, and politicians. It will be your job to bring about justice for all."

He raised his right arm and pointed his index finger at every row of desks in front of him. "Don't be slackers!"

He turned his back to his students and faced the flag of Cuba. "Now, my sons, salute your country and its new leaders."

Francisco stood with his chest inflated and held his salute a moment longer. I'm ready to do anything, he thought.

Brother Alfonso shouted, "You may not sit until I give permission!"

Francisco turned slightly to see who would dare move a muscle without Remache allowing it — it was Roberto, of course — and he caught the eye of his best friend Arturo. He was stifling a laugh.

The 4:15 bell rang and Francisco raced for the classroom door. Once outside, he waited for Arturo. He felt a strong grip on his shoulder and turned to find his tall, lean, chocolate-colored friend. There was no other friend with whom Francisco felt as relaxed as he did with Arturo. He had two other close friends, and many not-so-close ones, but, in spite of their physical differences, Arturo was the most like him. Next to his family, it was Arturo he could count on: They made an odd pair, but they were like brothers.

Arturo was by far the best baseball player on the school team, and everyone expected him to play professionally. Francisco played, too, but just hoped to get out of the dugout. That afternoon, he planned to ask Arturo for help catching a low ball and getting it to first base without losing his balance.

After they reached the locker room, Arturo wrapped his foot around Francisco's leg, threw him to the floor, and laughed. Francisco jumped up, charged, and rammed his friend into his locker door before collapsing in laughter on a bench.

January 19, 1959

$\mathcal{F}$rancisco had not forgotten the salute Fidel had given him when he emerged from the crowd and longed to see his face again. According to *La Marina*, Fidel was now head of the military and had established his home and office in the penthouse of the Hilton Hotel. Instead of walking the ten blocks directly to his house after baseball practice as he had promised his mother he would do, Francisco turned down Thirteenth Street toward Presidents' Avenue. There he took a bus to Twenty-third where he got off and jumped on another. A soldier stood on every corner of this street holding a rifle.

The crowded bus slowed when it neared the Hilton Hotel but didn't stop. Surprised that it didn't, Francisco realized that he wouldn't have been able to get out anyway because soldiers packed the sidewalk, shoulder to shoulder, in front of the wide glass doors of the new, ultra-modern hotel. When the bus slowed at the corner of M and Twenty-third, he jumped to the sidewalk, scraping his knees on the rough cement. He brushed off his pants and walked to the closest building where he edged along until he reached the corner opposite the hotel. There he waited fifteen minutes, trying to decide what to do, before approaching the youngest-looking soldier he could find.

"Is he in there?" Francisco asked, pointing toward the hotel.

At first, the soldier acted like he didn't hear Francisco, then he turned to face him. "What? You mean our leader? Sure he is. He's working."

Francisco was careful not to bump the rifle. "They allowing anyone in? Could I see him? Or where he works?"

The young man laughed. "Kid, we're protecting him from people like you — rich Batista people in their uniforms. Now, get away." He grasped his gun with both hands and nudged Francisco with its handle.

Francisco wanted to protest, but I am not rich, and in my family, we hate Batista. But instead he slipped behind another soldier and crossed the street. He saw that buses still weren't stopping in this area of Twenty-third, so he ran the six blocks to Malecón Boulevard, slowing down enough to think about the soldier's words when he reached the enormous Nacional Hotel. He regarded the wings of the Nacional that jutted in four directions and its two elegant towers. What the soldier said confused him but it had been noisy there, he thought, and maybe he didn't hear me.

Francisco crossed the Malecón at the corner and waited at the bus stop across the street from the Maine Monument. Waves crashed against the seawall behind him. It comforted him to see the structure that his Uncle Bernardo had designed.

The Maine Monument commemorated the sinking of the American battleship, Maine, and the loss of two hundred sixty-six American sailors in Havana harbor in 1898 during the Cuban War of Independence. Its twin marble columns stood side by side representing equal partners in friendship, Cuba and the United States. "Libertad" was inscribed on a lintel above the columns. Atop that was a three-ton bronze eagle, its great wings outstretched, symbolizing again the friendship between the two countries. In the center of its marble base was a plaque inscribed: "Joint resolution: The people of the Island of Cuba Are and of Right Ought to be Free and Independent. Congress of the United States, April, 1898." The names of the dead sailors were listed on the base. Two ten-inch-cannons recovered from the ship were set perpendicular to the columns.

The next bus was crowded but slowed and allowed Francisco to squeeze in. On his way home, he tried to think of something to tell his mother that wouldn't get him into too much trouble.

Francisco unlocked the door to his family's building and went inside. The door to his father's orthopedic office was closed, so it must be after seven, he thought. Mami will kill me.

But no one greeted him except his sister who was lying on the living-room couch reading and watching television, her curly brown hair spread over the arm of the couch. "Mami and Papy are with Tía Julia and Tío Eduardo in Tía Elena's living room," she said without turning her head. "Something's wrong."

Francisco hurried down the hall to his bedroom, dropped onto his bed, and looked at the clock. It was seven-thirty. I'll find out soon, he thought. Dinner's in half an hour.

Francisco's mother's siblings, except for her brother Carlos, lived in four three-story buildings that filled an entire block. His parents' apartment was on the right corner, connected to the building on its left by an interior stairway. That building belonged to two of his mother's sisters, Elena and Juanita. It was connected to the building on its left, owned by sister Julia and her husband, Eduardo.

A free-standing building to their left belonged to their brother, Bernardo, a well-known architect. He had designed the buildings so each sister could rent out two of the floors to supplement their incomes.

Francisco's family lived on their third floor and rented out two apartments on the second and one on the first, adjacent to his father's medical office.

The door connecting his parents' building to his aunts' was in Francisco's bedroom. He lay on his bed, wondering what could be wrong, when his mother and father came through that door at 7:59. That they hadn't knocked surprised the boy until he saw his mother's red, swollen eyes and his father's angry face.

"Come to dinner," his father growled.

Francisco knew this wasn't the time for questions. He followed his parents down the hall.

Luisa moved the book she had propped open on the glass dining table when her parents approached, just as Rosa brought in a platter of carne asada. No one spoke as they ate the grilled beef and rice until Rosa collected the empty dinner plates and brought in the guava jam and cream cheese for dessert.

"Tío Eduardo's bank account has been frozen by our new government," Francisco's father said.

Luisa asked, "What does that mean?"

Her father sighed and looked down at his dessert plate. "Right now, he can't use the money he has in the bank." He slapped the table and leaned back in his chair. "Unbelievable! He can't withdraw any of his own money!"

"But why?" Luisa asked.

He shook his head. "The bank president didn't want to say much, but he did ask about Eduardo's brother's financial dealings with Batista's friends. Eduardo was in a land-development group with them, though he got out years ago. Wouldn't you think they'd trust a man who's been director of the National Institutes of Health?" He tossed his napkin on the table and stood. "Well, they'll get it straightened out. They still have income from their apartment rentals."

Francisco turned to his mother. "So did they take his brother's money, too, Mami?"

"He left," she said, curling her lips. "I'm sure his money is in a bank outside the country. He has a house in Miami and who knows what else. Same with his friends. Lots of money there."

Francisco left the table and hurried down the hall to his room knowing from whom he could learn more — Tía Elena. He picked up his physics and trigonometry books and started down the spiral stairs to her second-floor apartment. As both his godmother and former school-teacher, she enjoyed sitting with him while he did his homework in her living room. Theirs had always been a special relationship. Francisco often wondered if he felt so close to her because she looked so much like his mother or because he spent more time with her than any other adult.

He knocked softly before opening his godmother's living-room door. She was in her sky-blue wing-back chair across from the couch, and she looked up at him, beaming. Her knitting basket was on the floor beside her and she held her knitting needles in mid-row of a wool vest in Francisco's school colors. On the carved wooden table in front of her was a plate of chocolate-chip cookies.

"Here you are, mi Panchito — my little Pancho. Much homework tonight?"

Francisco dropped his books on the table, picked up a cookie and a napkin, and slumped down on the couch. "Tía, will Tío Eduardo get his money back?"

His aunt laid her knitting needles aside, moved to the couch, and hugged him. "Oh, mi hijo, don't worry. That money is nothing. Tío Eduardo and Tía Julia will be fine. All of us have our homes and our family — that's what matters!"

The next day Francisco waved goodbye to Arturo at the school gate and headed down Thirteenth Street to El Vedado Tennis Club. Now that football season was over, along with his responsibilities as captain of the football team, he could go there every day except when there was baseball practice at school. With six tennis courts, a baseball

stadium and softball field, three swimming pools, an outdoor basketball court, and a bowling alley, there was plenty
to keep him busy. That morning at breakfast his mother had
told him to work on his tennis. "You can use some practice
on your serve, hijo! I'll be watching for more power and ac-
curacy at your next match!"

A flatbed truck carrying twenty or so teen-agers sporting the beginnings of beards came up Thirteenth. One was
waving the red, white, and blue Cuban flag, another shouted something about becoming soldiers, and others chanted,
"Fidel, Fidel." Why do we need more soldiers, he asked
himself. The revolution is over. When the truck passed,
Francisco spotted an ice-cream vendor's cart. He crossed
the street, and bought a cone of soft chocolate.

The tennis club, on Twelfth and Calzada Streets beside
the mouth of the Almendares River, was bordered on three
sides by an intricate cement wall that reminded Francisco
of the white lace doilies on the tables in his grandmother's
house. He pushed aside the sprawling crimson bougainvillea vine that draped over it to see whether the courts were
full and hoped his friend, Roberto, was free to play. But
Roberto wasn't on the courts. He slipped his handkerchief
from his pants pocket, wiped the sweat from his face and
forehead, and turned into the circular drive. He glanced at
the Greek statue of the discus-thrower in the center of the
drive, and sighed. Exercise would never make him that fit.

Having been reprimanded by a few of his mother's
friends for running inside the building, Francisco walked
slowly from the foyer through the trophy room, stopping
to scan the bulletin board, and continuing on to the terrace

where he looked around for Roberto. The strong breeze rustling the palm fronds was cool enough to convince him that his friend wouldn't be swimming. As he wandered around the first floor, he momentarily considered climbing the marble stairway to the second or third floors but didn't see the point since only the adult facilities were there. He turned back toward the teen boys' locker room to change before going outside.

He saw a large group of boys gathered at the outdoor bar. That was unusual, because, though it was legal for teenagers to drink alcohol, generally they didn't at the club. So Francisco headed in that direction. Thirty or so people — mostly teenagers with Roberto among them — surrounded a man dressed in navy pants and a long-sleeved white shirt. They grasped his hands and patted him on the back. The younger boys were dancing playfully around him. When Francisco reached the group he recognized the man at the center of attention. It was Señor García — the former Vedado District police chief who had left his post eight months before. It was rumored that he had led a group of Havana policemen and university students against Batista's secret police. They had set bombs and sabotaged their activities.

Francisco made his way through the crowd and laid his hand on the man's arm. "Señor, you're home."

Señor García turned to him and smiled. "Good to see you Francisco. How's your father?" He put his arm around Francisco's shoulder. "It all ended just right, didn't it?"

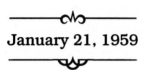

January 21, 1959

"Students, attention!" Brother Alfonso stood beside his mahogany desk. "Stop talking immediately."

Francisco was talking to his friend, Virgilio, but stopped midsentence and turned to face his teacher. He's upset, he thought. That slight stutter — when he does that, he's always upset.

"At the beginning of every day," Brother Alfonso said, "I will call to your attention new government decisions and events in our country. It is extremely important to our fledgling democracy that you be an informed citizenry. I will elaborate when I feel explanation is necessary. Our provisional president, Manuel Urrutia, who was appointed by Che Guevara three weeks ago, has issued a directive that all political parties be banned. This is only temporary, however, since multiparty elections will be held in eighteen months.

"Second, Congress has been dismissed and all members elected in 1954 and 1958 are barred from holding office again. Third, labor unions, because they were powerful supporters of the former dictator, are banned. And last, the United States Military Assistance Group has been expelled from the country." Brother Alfonso paused and lowered his voice. "Our leadership says it wants a good relationship with our northern neighbor but not a dependent one."

He pursed his lips and lowered his head before continuing. "Boys, we must pray for the future of our country."

Francisco was confused. Brother Alfonso seemed upset, but why? Elections were to be held in eighteen months. Wouldn't a democratic vote straighten it all out? Nothing would be banned at that point.

February 1959

*F*rancisco struggled to button the trousers of his blue suit. He dreaded having to tell his mother that his clothes were getting tight, though she had probably noticed. His father had been complaining about the medical school and college expenses for his brothers at Tulane, and expressed his hope that the University of Havana would reopen in the fall. Ramón could go there his third year and it would cost them nothing. At least my parents won't have to throw a big party for me the way they did for Luisa's fifteenth birthday three years ago, he thought.

He tugged on the knot of his tie to loosen it. He looked in the mirror over his dresser, smoothed down his thick hair, and grinned. Today was his birthday, February first. It was a big one, his fifteenth. He, his parents, and his sister were going to mass, and then to Abuela de Twenty-one's house for a birthday lunch. His father's sisters, Clara and Regina, and Tía Sofia would be there, and he was certain Tía Clara would make the orange cake he loved. After that, he would meet Roberto at the club.

Francisco didn't call his mother for a ride home from the club, instead he walked, stopping to catch his breath on the way up the two flights of stairs. Something was making him tired, and it wasn't the baseball game or the walk home. When he opened the living-room door, he saw that the folding table had been set up at the end of the dining table. Both tables were covered with lace tablecloths and his mother's best china and silver. Ten Waterford crystal champagne glasses stood on a silver tray on the buffet. He smiled and called, "Mami! Who's coming? Will Tío Bernardo be here?"

Silvia came out of the kitchen wearing a light gray wool dress, her medium-length pearls, and an apron. The soft curls of her gray-streaked dark brown hair framed her smiling face. She hugged her youngest son. "Feliz cumpleaños — happy birthday, again, mi hijo. And yes, your aunts and uncles all wanted to celebrate with you. Rosa volunteered to work today so we could do it. Just for you!"

Tío Bernardo and his wife, Raquel, were the first to arrive. Francisco was especially glad he had come because he loved the way his uncle thought. His opinions were out of the ordinary, and you never knew what he would come up with next. He also laughed at Francisco's wisecracks.

The dinner table was quieter than usual: No one interrupted or talked louder than anyone else. No one tried to convince anyone else that his ideas were better. Everyone complimented Rosa's chicken with onions and garlic, and her black beans, too, but said little else.

Francisco was seated next to Bernardo at the table. He

40

turned to face him and smiled. "Oye — hey, I have a new joke for you."

"Let's hear it," his uncle said half-heartedly.

After polite laughter, silence again descended on the table.

When Luisa left the table to go to the bathroom, Francisco decided to try something. He excused himself, left the room, and hid around the corner, out of sight.

Just as he expected, the tables lit up, buzzing with talk. Five minutes later, he stepped back into the room and the talking stopped. Something was going on and it didn't seem fair to him to be kept in the dark. I'm an adult now, he thought.

When Francisco returned home from baseball practice on Monday, the TV was on in the living room, although no one was watching it. He paused to let the images register. Three men sat behind a desk and a single man sat in front of it. Francisco got down on his knees in front of the set to see more clearly. The men behind the desk were dressed alike in the olive-green uniforms he had seen all over town except that the man in the center wore a beret with a red star pinned to the front. Che Guevara, he's still here? Wonder why he hasn't gone home to Argentina now that the revolution's over?

Francisco listened.

"I followed orders but never arrested innocent people or tortured anyone. Never! I would not. Believe me!" The

41

lone man in front of the desk leaned forward and spoke with a strained voice.

The three men at the desk looked down at the paperwork in front of them and then at each other.

"Colonel, you are sentenced to death by firing squad," Che said. Two soldiers approached, seized the colonel by his upper arms and dragged him out of the room as he yelled, "No, stop. I want a lawyer!"

Francisco dropped his book bag, sat down where he had been kneeling, and fixed his eyes on the television screen. The same scene was repeated with a sergeant and a captain. "You are accused and found guilty of betraying your country, and are sentenced to death," each was told in short order and dragged away off-camera.

"But, why? What did I do? Where's the judge and jury?" the men screamed.

The picture shifted to an inner patio in La Cabaña prison where a row of soldiers with rifles stood. The men declared guilty were led onto the patio and placed in front of a dark stone wall. Che lined up beside the soldiers and shouted, "Fire!" The three men in front of the wall jerked, dropped to the blood-spattered patio, and slumped over — two on their sides, one face forward. Che removed his pistol from its holster, walked toward them, and fired one shot in each of their temples. He turned and, like a walking mannequin, left the patio.

When the TV screen faded to black, Francisco stretched out on the floor, wiped his wet cheeks with his palm, and clutched his chest with his trembling arms.

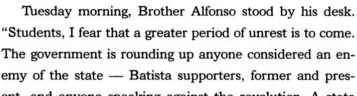

Tuesday morning, Brother Alfonso stood by his desk. "Students, I fear that a greater period of unrest is to come. The government is rounding up anyone considered an enemy of the state — Batista supporters, former and present, and anyone speaking against the revolution. A state must establish order," he paused, "but remember, killing is a grievous sin."

Now Francisco waited for the newspaper every morning but avoided the TV. Trials and executions were continuing, speeding up, it appeared to him. Raúl Castro, Fidel's younger brother, was now aiding Che in administering the last shot to the condemned man's head. The newspaper reported that many people were being arrested and tortured. The word, "Guilty!" was all it took to condemn a man to the wall or to twenty-to-thirty years in prison.

The front page of *Diario de la Marina* read, "Prime minister José Cardona resigns and leaves for exile in the U.S. Fidel appoints himself prime minister."

Brother Alfonso, standing at his desk once again, greeted his students. This time he was smiling. "There is good news today, boys. The government has responded to a protest by the restaurant, hotel, and casino workers who lost their jobs when the casinos were closed. Fidel has ordered them reopened, and has appointed himself president of the National Tourist Board. No protestor was arrested!"

"Oye, oye," Roberto whispered.

Francisco sat up straight, wondering how Roberto had the nerve to talk while Brother Alfonso was giving homework instructions. He put his finger to his lips but as soon as the 4:15 bell rang, he stood. "What?"

"Got a surprise," Roberto said. "Papy said he'd take us to some bars to celebrate your birthday. I've been working on him since I turned fifteen and he finally said OK!"

"Bars?" Francisco raised his eyebrows.

Roberto shook his head. "Well, not just any bar. I want to see Hemingway. Papy will take us to the places where he goes."

"I don't know if Mami will let me." She probably won't, he thought. "When is this?"

"Tomorrow night. Don't tell her where we're going. Just tell her you're staying with me."

The two boys climbed into Señor Montaño's new two-tone blue-and-white Mercury convertible Friday evening after dinner. The top was down. Francisco shivered in the cool air and looked up at the stars. It was strange to be in a car without a roof, and he wondered what would prevent them from falling out if Roberto's father had to stop quickly.

Señor Montaño was retired and at least fifteen years older than Francisco's father. When the horses were running, he was at the track. He wore a white suit no matter what the season. His tie this night was black and he had a black silk handkerchief in the breast pocket of his jacket.

His thick white hair was blown by the wind as soon as they got out on the road.

Their first stop was La Bodeguita del Medio in Old Havana. Señor Montaño told them it was a bohemian hangout known for its mojitos — drinks of rum, mint, lime juice, sugar and club soda. As the three entered, two guitarists and one maracas player were singing "Ojos Verdes — Green Eyes." Francisco looked around. The walls of the small bar and dining room were covered with photos of musicians, buildings, and famous people from around the world.

Roberto's father led the boys to a small round table, signaled a waiter, ordered three mojitos, and then turned to the boys. "This is where Hemingway comes for his mojitos. He used to live near here." He looked around and leaned back in the straight chair. "We'll wait awhile to see if Papa shows up. Slowly, now, boys. Only one drink."

Francisco had never heard of a mojito. He sipped and pursed his lips. Too tart, he thought. It won't be hard for me to make it last.

A woman in a tight red dress, a hibiscus flower pinned in her upswept hair, stood and danced. Her large round bottom swung from side to side as her partner caressed it. Francisco gulped his drink and stared.

After an hour they left.

"OK, boys, one more place. Hemingway's other favorite is La Floridita. That's where he drinks daiquiris."

The Old City was filled with people darting back and forth across the narrow streets in front of the many cars, making their fifteen blocks to the next bar slow going. But at least Francisco no longer felt the chill of the winter night.

La Floridita was larger and more elegant than Bodeguita. A long, curved mahogany bar stood in front of a mirror covering most of the wall and framed by four columns. The tops of the columns were intricately carved and heavily gilded. A chandelier holding multi-pointed, starry lights hung at each end of the bar.

Señor Montaño pointed to the white-padded vinyl stool around the far curve of the bar. "That's where he sits. A big man with white hair. I saw him once. OK, boys, this time we're sitting at the bar. Take a stool!"

Francisco and Roberto ordered traditional daiquiris, made with rum, lime juice, sugar, and maraschino liqueur, but Señor Montaño had a Papa Dobles, a grapefruit daiquiri created especially for Ernest "Papa" Hemingway.

An hour later, when Roberto slapped the bar and whooped, "Where is he, Papy? Why isn't he here?" his father paid the bill, slipped off his stool and led them laughing and talking to the car.

"Hijo, it's generous of Arturo's mother to invite you for a birthday lunch, but how will you find your way home? Neither of us knows these central Havana streets well." Silvia stopped her car, blocking a lane of traffic on the narrow street, and pointed. "Ask that man where the hotel is."

"He said, around the corner, Mami. On the right."

"And why are we going to the Lido Hotel?" she asked.

Francisco turned quickly to face his mother. "Mami, I told you three times. Arturo said it was easier to find than his building." He looked at his watch. "Hurry. I'm supposed to be there at 12:30."

"And you'll know which bus to take home?"

"Arturo takes these buses every day. He'll show me."

Francisco spotted his friend leaning against the wall beside the small wooden door of the hotel. "Here. Stop. I see him." When Silvia slowed the car, he jumped out and waved to her. He knew she had doubts about leaving him here, but she drove away.

Arturo pointed to the hotel. "This is where Mami works — on the cleaning staff."

A street vendor with pyramids of oranges and pineapples hanging from the sides of his two-wheeled wooden cart was parked along the path, causing them to step off the narrow sidewalk and into the street. Francisco noticed the cut-up mangoes and papayas, his favorites, and turned to Arturo. "Should we buy some fruit?"

"No, no!" Arturo grabbed his sleeve. "Mami has lunch ready. Come on."

When they turned the corner and passed three young women — one dressed in a short red skirt and two in long tight skirts with slits up the side — Francisco tapped his friend on the shoulder and swiveled around, continuing to stare. He was certain he could see through their blouses.

Arturo nodded and pointed, and said, "Un bayu — a whorehouse." The salsa music coming from the doorway drew Francisco's eye. He felt his friend pulling on his upper arm before he got a good look, though. "All right, I'm coming!"

Arturo nudged Francisco over to a high, wide-arched wooden door with metal studs around the edges and took

47

his keys from his pocket. Francisco stepped back to get a better look at the three-story building. The lower floor was blotched with patches of the white paint that had once covered it all. Narrow carved wooden balconies, painted blue like the front door, extended from the second- and third-floor windows. Arturo pointed to the second floor. "That's ours."

A blue-black-skinned woman grasped Francisco's hand. She was as tall as his father, six feet. A large smile framed her perfect white teeth and her warm brown eyes twinkled. "Arturito's friend! Another happy birthday to you. You are so welcome in our home."

The small living room was decorated in gold, bright pink, and deep blue. Music that made Francisco want to dance played in the background. Candles burned beside small statues on a corner cabinet. Fragrant aromas wafted from the kitchen. "Smells great in here, Señora. Is that cinnamon?"

Señora López nodded. "Arturito, show Francisco a seat." She turned toward the kitchen door.

Francisco peered out the large arched window onto the street before sitting down. "Man, must be fun living here. A lot going on down there."

Arturo grinned. "Yeah, it is, but not as much as usual. Not many tourists lately."

His mother returned with a platter of croquetas de jamón — ham croquettes. As she held them before Francisco, she turned to her son and motioned for him to get up. "Bring the glasses of orange juice for you and your friend."

Francisco took a deep breath and picked up a croquette. He held it a moment, remembering that his mother had forbidden him to eat them outside the house because she was afraid that people might prepare them with meat scraps instead of the well-cooked ham that she used. He glanced at the brown breadcrumbs covering the one-and-one-half-inch cylinder and popped the whole thing into his mouth.

"Sorry. I love these things." Then he picked up another.

Señora López set the platter on the round table in front of Francisco and sat down beside him. "Arturito told me you just had your fifteenth birthday. But most of the boys in your class are sixteen."

"I skipped the seventh grade."

"And you enjoy your class?"

"Oh, yes." He pointed to Arturo. "And this guy is getting ready for the major leagues."

Señora held up the platter and offered the boys another croquette. "My son has gone to the best school in Havana since fourth grade — he takes the bus forty minutes each way — and his grades are good, but all he thinks about is being a baseball player. You know he wants to go to the U.S. and play there after he graduates, don't you?"

Francisco nodded, his mouth full of croquette.

Señora López continued. "He may be counting too much on my aunt's husband's cousin. Did you know she's married to Conrado Marrero?"

Francisco gulped down the croquette he was chewing. "You mean Connie Marrero — El Curvo? The best baseball player in Cuba?"

Señora López nodded. "Yes, he and his wife met when they were both working in a department store. He worked there during the week and played for the Almendares team

49

on Sundays. He was twenty-seven before he became famous and left to play for the Washington Senators."

"You mean he'll help Arturo?" Francisco looked surprised as he turned to his friend. "Why didn't you tell me? You've got it made!"

Arturo shifted in his chair and muttered, "We're not sure."

"That's right," said his mother. "As I told Arturito, famous men have many people asking for favors and Conrado is retired now."

"But ... but, he's almost related to you," Francisco said. "And he coached for the Havana Sugar Kings. Has he seen you pitch?"

Arturo shook his head. "Mami's aunt's working on it."

"But what about you?" She turned to Francisco and flashed her enormous smile. "What will you do after graduation?"

"I want to be a lawyer. Like my grandfather."

Arturo's mother stood. "Maybe you can convince Arturito to go to university, too. Let's go to the kitchen."

The boys sat down at a round table big enough for four and covered with a green, orange, and red-striped cloth. Señora López placed a platter of another of Francisco's favorite foods before him — picadillo with rice. The spicy, sweet ground beef mixture with peppers, onions, olives, and raisins was surrounded by green peas and sprinkled with chopped hard-boiled egg.

Francisco felt his mouth water and reminded himself of his mother's words: Don't eat so fast, and don't talk with food in your mouth.

To finish the meal, Señora López brought a shimmering coconut flan to the table. Francisco turned to Arturo. "Does she cook like this all the time?"

Arturo nodded. "When she's not working."

After lunch, Señora López insisted that her son walk Francisco to the bus stop. Francisco accepted without protesting because, like his mother, he wasn't familiar with this part of the city.

The city of Havana lies, east to west, with its northern border along the Straits of Florida and the eastern one beside the Bay of Havana. The bay is a narrow inlet dividing into three fingers, each with its own harbor.

Perched atop a two-hundred-foot limestone ridge across the entrance to the bay stands a fortification, Castillo de los Trés Reyes Magos del Morro — commonly known as Morro Castle — built by the Spanish in 1589 to provide protection from pirates. Its lighthouse tower rises one hundred feet and can be seen for miles. On a platform are twelve cannons called the twelve apostles.

The easternmost section of the city, built by the Spanish in 1519, is Old Havana. The city spread westward as it grew, creating central Havana where Arturo and his mother lived, and, west of that, the Vedado suburb where Francisco lived.

"You in a hurry?" Francisco asked his friend.

Arturo shook his head, no. "What's on your mind?"

"I'd like to walk around. See what's here."

"This way." Arturo pointed as he turned left.

Francisco heard men laughing and arguing, smelled cigar smoke, and knew they were near a dominoes game before he saw it.

51

The grassy park was just big enough for four concrete game tables and two jacaranda trees. Their lacy branches created patches of shade that shifted lazily in the breeze.

The boys stopped a few feet from a table where four men were playing. "You ever play?" Francisco pointed to the board.

Arturo shook his head. "Never been that interested, and don't know how."

Francisco turned to face his friend. "What? How can a Cuban not know dominoes?" He pointed to the table. "Look at them — four men, two on a team — playing with fifty-five tiles. Dots range zero to nine. You have to place a tile with the same number that's on one of the ends, or you draw. When someone goes out, the points in your hand count against you. They play three sets to one hundred or one hundred fifty points. The team taking two sets wins. Seems like everybody in the country plays, but I don't either, actually." He slapped his friend on the shoulder. "Maybe we're too busy looking at girls."

"Me pegue! — I stuck it!" called the victorious man in the jipijapa, a finely woven straw hat with a black band, as he placed the winning tile. He reached across the table and smacked his palm against his partner's. He groaned as he stood, smoothing some of the wrinkles from his white guayabera, and motioned for the man standing behind him to take his place.

A gray-haired woman sitting on a bench beside the game table applauded. Francisco noticed that her upper and lower front teeth were missing, so she had her cigar clamped between her back teeth on the left side of her mouth.

The winner removed his hat and bowed in her direction. She clapped again.

The boys moved on.

"Look," Francisco said, pointing to a group gathered on the corner ahead. "Come on!" He sped up. "Guarapo. I love cane juice. I'm buying."

Francisco and Arturo waited behind the vendor, watching him stuff the peeled sugarcane into the juicer, then crank the handle. When the liquid sugar filled a cup, he squeezed half a lime into it, plopped in a straw, and passed it to his next customer.

The boys wove in and out of the crowds as they sipped their juice. Francisco focused on lowering his head, worried that he could bump it on the iron filigree balconies hanging over the narrow sidewalks. He glanced at his watch. "Uh-oh. Four o'clock. Gotta hurry."

They were breathing hard when they reached the Plaza de Armas — parade ground. Francisco's eyes widened. "This is great." He turned to Arturo. "My uncle Bernardo brought me here when I was seven. He and another guy designed the renovation of this place to make it look like it did when it was built. I love this place! You know this is the spot where Havana was founded, don't you?" He pointed. "And look, there's the fortress the Spanish built to keep pirates out."

Francisco stumbled on the uneven cobblestones as he walked toward the moat surrounding the fortress. He looked down into the dirty water and then up at the tower in front of him. On top was a weathervane in the shape of a woman.

"Wow. I should come here more often. Look at the old

Presidential Palace. Built by the Spaniards in the 1700s until we chased them out. And there's the Temple." Then Francisco laughed. "Sorry. You don't need a tour guide, do you?" He looked at his watch again. "Mami will kill me! Gotta go. Where do I get a bus?"

"We're near Céspedes." Arturo pointed. "Let's go to that stop and it'll take you home by the Malecón. Won't take long."

Francisco finally got on a bus that would take him home. As it continued up Carlos M. Céspedes Avenue and past the bronze statue of General Máximo Gómez on horseback atop a white marble pedestal, Francisco remembered his history lessons: Gómez had led his country in two wars of independence, and Céspedes became the father of the country by freeing his own slaves in 1868 and starting the Ten Years' War against Spain.

Francisco ran up the stairs of his home, collapsing in his seat at the dining table just as his parents were sitting down to dinner. His mother raised her eyebrows. "So long? It must have been quite a lunch."

"Sorry, Mami, but we walked over to Plaza de Armas and looked around. I had a great time."

Luisa hung up the phone, and slipped into her chair at the table.

"You're late," Papy said to her.

"Sorry, Papy. I was waiting for Isabel's father to decide about the truck. He said yes, he'll rent one for us to ride on the first afternoon of Carnaval. One of those flatbed things that holds ten."

"Who's Isabel?" Francisco asked.

"Girl at my school."

"Isabel Ferro Pidal," Papy replied. "And her father can certainly afford to rent a truck for a night. For many nights, in fact."

"Who will drive it?" her mother asked. "And what about your costumes? It'll be just the first night, won't it? Not the whole week?"

"Their chauffeur will drive. We're going to be circus clowns just fooling around — juggling and throwing those curled paper streamers. We'll line the front with helium balloons."

"That sounds wonderful!" Silvia leaned forward and laid her hand over her daughter's. "Eat, now, dear."

Francisco's mother and father parked behind the Inglaterra Hotel across from Central Park, and Francisco hopped out of the car. "Mami, I have to meet Roberto at the Martí statue in the park."

"Zip up your jacket. It's cold. Feels like rain."

Francisco ran across Havana's most elegant street, the Prado, and through Central Park, weaving around palm trees and costumed people. He spotted his friend sitting on the steps of the grand marble statue dedicated to José Martí, an advocate for universal equality, democracy, and freedom, and a national hero. He waved when he caught Roberto's eye.

"Oye!" Francisco said when he reached him. "Have you ever seen the statue of Martí in New York's Central Park?"

Roberto stood and shook his head, no.

"I saw it when I was six," Francisco said. "It's huge! He's on a horse right at the entrance to the park. I understand why it's in New York since he escaped his exile in Spain and moved there, but what I don't get is why he's on a horse. He was a writer, not a military man." He hesitated before adding, "Strange, though, that he was killed in battle."

A woman wearing a blue eye-mask lined with silver sequins and a skin-tight, low-cut white dress grasped Roberto's hand. "Let's go watch the parade, good-lookin'."

Roberto jerked his hand away, and rolled his eyes at Francisco.

Francisco punched him in the back and then stroked his friend's hair. "Oh, handsome, what can you do for me?" he said in falsetto. They bent over and giggled so hard they had to hold their sides.

The boys ran on, dodging vendors' carts selling popcorn and masks. Francisco spotted his mother and father, waved to them, and sat down on the curb beside Roberto. He was about to search for the churros he smelled coming from his left when he heard the drums and jumped up.

In a straight line spanning the street, twenty black men were beating tall, narrow, single-headed conga drums and the double-headed hourglass bata drums from Africa. Their skin shone as if it had been oiled. Behind them another line of men played cornets and saxophones. The third line shook maracas. All were dressed in pants and long-sleeved shirts of shimmering blue-and-pink-striped silk. Behind them four men balanced the traditional farolas — eight-foot-high lampposts with lanterns on top — tucked into a cup connected to a leather strap around their waists. Pastel crinkled paper streamers flowed about them.

The La Sultana Comparsa — club — had sponsored the queen for this first night of Carnaval. Her throne was on a platform at the end of her float. She wore a tiara and a long, flowing white gown. In front of her were six giant swan carriages ferrying the ladies of her court. Francisco whistled.

After the queen came groups in elaborate costumes performing choreographed music and dances they had rehearsed for nearly a year. Others, dressed in a multitude of colors, styles, and fabrics, rode in convertibles and waved. One float held a replica of a ship with the people aboard dressed as pirates.

"Hey, Luisa! Luisa, here!" Francisco and Roberto shouted, waving their arms as the flatbed truck approached. Luisa's soft brown curls swayed with the movement of the truck as she threw narrow paper streamers into the crowd. Francisco was struck by the sweet smile that reminded him of their mother's. Luisa and her friends had painted their faces white and their noses red. They wore red, white, and blue polka-dot jumpsuits. Three of the girls juggled small red and white balls, and two swayed to keep hula hoops circling their bodies.

"Oye." Francisco elbowed Roberto. "Look at the size of those horses. Bet we couldn't even get up on one." Carriages filled with men in ornate Spanish uniforms pulled by teams of sleek, dark-brown horses sporting silver harnesses brought the parade to a close. "Come on, let's go see the fireworks."

April 1959

*I*nstead of going to the club Wednesday after school, Francisco waited at the bus stop on Thirteenth Street to go home. He had been avoiding television so he wouldn't be faced by the executions, but Fidel was on his way to Washington, D.C., and Francisco wanted to see how Americans reacted to him. He was getting mixed messages at home about Fidel. Tío Eduardo felt they should be patient and give the government a chance to move toward democracy, whereas his father had no trust in him at all. Francisco was frustrated but didn't know what a person his age could do except wait.

Fidel had been invited to speak at a conference of the American Society of Newspaper Editors on April fifteenth. It would be the beginning event in an eleven-day, six-city tour across the eastern U.S. and Canada called "Operation Truth." According to *La Marina*, his intent was to explain what free Cubans wanted from their government and to dispel suspicions of his motives.

The TV was already on when Francisco opened the living-room door, the announcer describing Fidel's arrival at National Airport. "In spite of the pouring rain, hundreds have been waiting for hours to see him. Now they're chanting, 'Viva, Fidel!' Secret Service agents are frantic, trying to prevent him from pushing into the crowd, but he can't be stopped. He's reaching for the people. They love him!"

Francisco stood erect, and saluted. Look at that, he thought. Nothing to worry about: Americans think he's great.

The Thursday morning newspaper reported that the leader of free Cuba was being received warmly wherever he went. Americans cheered Fidel when he ate hot dogs at the National Zoo, and they held out their babies for him to kiss when he laid a wreath by the Washington Monument. The article continued. "A delegation from the U.S. State Department met with Fidel and offered expertise and loans. We are reminded that they provided him with arms when he was fighting in the mountains. But this time he asked only for private investment in dollars."

Then, on Page 2, Francisco read: "Government stops Catholic students from conducting literacy classes for soldiers." That makes no sense, he thought. What's wrong with a Catholic youth group teaching people how to read? Nearly everyone in this country is a Catholic.

May 18, 1959

*F*rancisco trudged up the stairs to his family's home, tired from a baseball game at the tennis club and bleeding from a scraped elbow. When he stepped into the living room, he was surprised to see his mother and father sitting at the dining table with Tía Julia and Tío Eduardo. His uncle was tapping on the glass table with his middle finger. "In the long run, this will be a good thing. The poor in the countryside have to be lifted up, and they can't do it by themselves." He pushed aside his espresso cup and leaned back.

Tío Eduardo's words carried weight. He was married to Francisco's mother's oldest sister and had been a confidant of her father who, as a retired Supreme Court justice, had been highly respected in the family and in the country. Eduardo himself was now retired after a varied and successful career. He was educated in chemistry and pharmacology and had been director of the National Institute of Health under President Machado. He had a profitable distillery business for ten years in New Orleans, and had travelled extensively. In short, he was a charming, brilliant man whose opinions were difficult to refute.

His wife, Julia, turned toward Francisco. "Ah, mi Panchito, come and join us. We're talking about the new Agrarian Reform Law." She gave Silvia a questioning look, and stood. "Let me get you some ice cream."

Francisco sat down beside his father, picked up one of the small croissant-shaped pastries from the plate in front of him, and bit into it. Umm, guava paste, he thought: my favorite. After swallowing the first bite of his coconut ice cream, he said, "Brother Alfonso announced the news this morning but didn't tell us much. What will happen?"

Silvia stood and pulled the chain on the living room ceiling fan until it reached the highest setting.

His father grumbled, "Trouble, if you ask me." He turned toward Francisco. "The government has decreed that no one is allowed to have a farm or ranch of more than one hundred caballerías — three thousand three hundred eleven acres. Any more than that and it will be taken and given to the poor."

His father went on to tell him that, supposedly, two hundred thousand people would receive land in sixty-seven-acre parcels and that foreigners couldn't own any land, not even their own sugar plantations. "What do you think the Americans will say to that?" he asked.

Francisco's father shifted in his chair and regarded his brother-in-law. "And guess what they pay you when they steal your land? Currency bonds with four-and-a-half percent interest after twenty years." He slapped the glass table and added that as a final insult, Fidel had also made himself president of the National Institute of Agrarian Reform, with a one hundred thousand-man militia to grab the land.

Eduardo countered, "Well, I know what you're thinking." He stubbed out his cigarette in the ashtray. "Yes, my bank account is still frozen. But we all believed something had to be done about poverty in the countryside. Let's give this land reform a chance."

June 1959

$\mathcal{F}$rancisco read the headlines of the June ninth morning newspaper that lay on the dining room table —
"Trafficante arrested/All casinos closed." The mob leader in
Cuba and Florida and owner of the Sans Souci Casino had
apparently found his comeuppance.

Francisco had hoped Brother Alfonso would explain why,
but instead his teacher announced more important chang-
es. "Boys, this is a true social and economic revolution. All
business and industry have been nationalized. Food, housing, health, transportation, electricity, and sugar production
are now owned and run by the state.

"Think about it: You may no longer own a shoe store or
a grocery store. They now belong to the government." He
elaborated that one goal was to a more even distribution
of housing. Rents would be controlled. Homes and properties owned by citizens who had left Cuba would be taken
over and owned by the government. Prices were supposed
to decrease. Brother Alfonso's speech slowed as he looked

toward a large open window and concluded: "This is a real shift."

At 4:15, Francisco rushed to the door of the classroom and waited in the hall for Arturo. "Hey, man, I think I'm ready for our game today." He raised his arm. "Feel these muscles."

Arturo half-heartedly punched his friend's upper arm and drifted down the hallway toward the gymnasium.

Francisco followed. "What's going on? You all right?"

Arturo shrugged. "Mami's worried about her job. Tourists aren't coming anymore."

Francisco slumped down on a bench in the locker room. "None of them?"

Arturo shook his head, no. "Especially not the Americans. Street in front of my house is empty."

In addition to their own school exams, private school students were required by the Cuban Department of Education to take the same end-of-year exams as public school students to make sure they were at the same level of knowledge and skill.

The Friday morning before lunch, Brother Alfonso announced, "Class, your public exams will be held in the Education Administration Building downtown Monday. You will be excused from class that morning. I advise you to study this weekend."

Francisco heard Roberto groan. When the bell rang for lunch, he turned around. "What's with you?"

"You know. We're both invited to Sarah's party Saturday night."

Francisco stood. "Yeah, well. Can't go now. You heard what Brother Alfonso said."

Roberto grabbed his friend's arm on the way down the hall. "But I heard this year's exams don't cover the first part of the year, just the second half. You remember all that stuff."

Francisco shook his head and laughed. His friend barely scraped by in class and was always making excuses for not studying. "You're kidding yourself."

"What about the races Sunday after mass. Going there?"

The prefect blew the whistle, signaling they could leave the grounds. Francisco yelled over his shoulder as he ran for the bus to his grandmother's house for lunch, "No, and you'd better not, either."

The exam, as Francisco suspected, covered the entire year's studies. At 11:00, he had just finished the last question when he saw Roberto rise and turn in his folder, speaking briefly with the monitor, and leaving the room.

Francisco sprang from his seat, dropped his exam on the table, and caught up with Roberto in the hallway. "Hey, man, I'm impressed. You did study this weekend."

Roberto grimaced. "Not exactly. I went to the party and to the races. And I think I just screwed up." He exhaled. "I wrote beside my exam signature that I would like to be forgiven for some of my answers, because I'm an orphan of both mother and father and I need to pass so I can get a job to support my brother and sister."

Francisco slapped his friend on the back and grinned. "You didn't!"

Roberto looked down. "It's worse," he said. "I didn't notice the woman at the desk until I stood up. She's a friend of Mami's. When I handed in my exam she asked how Mami was. I said, 'Just fine,' and got out of there as fast as I could."

Francisco sat down in the hall beside his friend and laughed until tears came to his eyes.

"Students, this is our last day together. The thirty-four of you who remain in this classroom have worked hard," Brother Alfonso said, "in spite of our great upheaval. I will call your names according to your final grade for the year — highest first — and you will line up in that order."

When his name was called, Francisco tugged at his damp shirt and wiped the sweat from his face. He took his place behind Ricardo, who he knew would be first because he did nothing after school or on weekends but study.

"Whew," he said to himself when Arturo's name was called fifth. His friend had seemed distracted recently, and he was relieved to see he had kept up with his schoolwork.

Francisco glanced at the six large open windows. He was glad to be leaving the heat and pressure of the city for two months. It surprised him that when he invited Arturo to join his family at the farm for a week or two, his friend had shaken his head, and said, "Can't, well, maybe, not sure."

Although the farm was about sixty miles east of Havana, it was on the bus route to Varadero Beach. The bus also passed Matanzas, the city nearest the farm, making the farm easy to get to and close to both the beach and a good-sized town.

July 1959

$\mathcal{I}$t had been three hours since they left for the farm. Francisco's mother drove even slower than usual because Tía Julia was following in her car and she was afraid they would get separated. Francisco had given up asking her to speed up and had stopped talking to anyone in the car — his father, sister and even his brother, Ramón, who had finished his second year at Tulane and returned home the week before. He laid his head back against the seat, closed his eyes, and focused on the warm breezes coming in through the window. The air here smelled more like the ocean than in Havana, even though it collected humidity from the same waters.

Luisa poked him in the ribs with her elbow. "Wake up, lazy, we're here," she said.

Francisco straightened, looked to his left and hoped they hadn't yet passed the entrance gate. Seconds later he saw the sign. Two Indian heads, carved in rough dark wood and facing in opposite directions, framed the name, Guaybaque.

Francisco's Uncle Bernardo had given that name to the property to commemorate a Cacique Indian chief who had lived nearby when Spain established its colony on the island.

Francisco loved spending his summers at Guaybaque for many reasons: the ocean, his dog, deep-sea fishing, long boat rides, and his cousins. Less easy to describe were things like hearing stories about the family and the history of Cuba that he had memorized by now but never tired of hearing.

Perhaps because he was born in his maternal grandfather's large, elegant home on M Street in the Vedado district of Havana, and had lived there with his family — grandparents, two aunts, and one uncle — until he was eight and his grandparents had died, it was a special pleasure for Francisco to hear about his grandfather. Although he had been addressed as Judge Soler, his full name was Bernardo José Soler Horta. As was the custom in Cuba, his father's family name, Soler, was placed first, followed by his mother's family name, Horta. He was known as Papa Grande by everyone in the family.

Papa Grande, born in 1858 in Matanzas, Cuba, was the most admired member of the family, and an unusual man. When ready to attend the university, he went to Barcelona, Spain, near where his father had been born in Sant Feliu de Guíxols on the Costa Brava. He played billiards so well that when he ran out of money for law school, he competed to support himself. After other players in the area had stopped betting against him, he traveled to surrounding towns to challenge the unsuspecting. When he finished his law degree, he returned to Matanzas, married, and established a law practice.

In 1896, Papa Grande was a strong supporter of Cuba's second insurrection against Spain, so the Spanish government exiled him and his family to Mexico. They returned to Cuba when the Cuban War of Independence/Spanish-American War ended, and he was appointed to the interim government established by the United States. He was made secretary to the leader of the Cuban army, General Máximo Gómez, and, in 1903, was appointed to the Supreme Court by Cuban President Estrada Palma. Eventually he became chief justice, and remained so for twenty-five years until his retirement.

Papa Grande was a guitar player, a poet, and a loving grandfather. It was because of Francisco's admiration for him and knowing him during the last four years of his grandfather's life that Francisco determined to become a lawyer, even though he feared he might not measure up to the older man's achievements.

Papa Grande bought Guaybaque — a country place of eight hundred fifty acres — and created a family compound, inviting all seven of his children to build summer homes there. When hunting with friends on his farm, Papa Grande wore a specially-designed jacket, but when fishing, he wore his usual black three-piece suit and tie. A fisherman would row him out, place bait on several hooks and hand him the rod. As soon as Papa Grande felt a pull on more than one hook, he handed the lines back to the fisherman to remove the fish from their hooks.

After Papa Grande and his wife died, Francisco's mother and her five living siblings — two brothers and three sisters — inherited Guaybaque. She and her family, along with the three sisters and one brother-in-law, spent their summers in the main house. Her second brother, Carlos, built a four-bedroom stone house with a red-tile roof that faced the bay for his wife and seven children.

But the talk of the coast was the building created by her older brother, Bernardo. Designed to look like the remaining turret of a castle in ruins — a taste of Old Europe — the three-story turret was built of stone, with a living room and kitchen off to the side. The first floor was used as an office and the second and third floors had one bedroom each. The house was placed on the end of a tiny peninsula extending into the bay and was referred to by his family, fishermen, and swimmers in the Bay of Matanzas as el castillo.

Off to the right of the main house and its kitchen extension was a one-story white stucco house built for the year-round caretaker and his family. Its front door was painted blue to remind him of the house in the city of Trinidad where he was born. Humberto looked after the horses and boats and cooked for those staying in the main house.

Francisco's mother steered the Chrysler left and then right down a colonnade of laurel trees in an attempt to avoid deep holes in the dirt driveway. When she reached the porch wrapped around the front and sides of the wood and stone two-story house, she brought the car to a stop. Francisco jumped out and ran toward the front door.

"Stop!" Silvia called. "Come back and unload the car. You can go to the beach when that's done."

Francisco and Ramón grabbed their suitcases and raced each other up the stairs to their second-floor bedroom and went back to the car and pulled a large cardboard box from the trunk. They carried it through the living room and across the breezeway that connected the main house to the kitchen and the three servants' rooms. Two more trips to the car released them from their mother's watch.

Francisco had packed his bathing suit on top of his other clothes so he could pull it on right away. He ran toward the bay. He stumbled on steps that Tío Bernardo had carved into the steep hillside and had to slow down. When he neared the bottom, he jumped, landing in the silky white sand. He splashed through warm water and sat down on the end of the pier. While waiting for his brother, he watched needlefish swimming in the clear water and tiny crabs crawling on the rocks. As he lay down on his stomach on the hot cement, he kept an eye out for the dreaded moray eels. They hid in crevices of the coral that supported the cement slab. Thinking of their glistening, inch-long teeth made him shiver.

"What are you lying there for? Let's go!" Ramón shouted as he bounded down the steps and headed for Tía Elena's twelve-foot rowboat that was tied to the pier.

On Sunday morning, Francisco's mother sat on the side of his bed and shook his shoulder. She called to Ramón. "Boys, Papy and I will be back for lunch on Saturday. Then I'll have five weeks off. Listen to your aunts and be on time for lunch and dinner." She stood and kissed each of them on their cheeks. "You know the rules. Tío Carlos will be gone, too. And probably Tío Bernardo."

Every year, Silvia and Pedro left the boys for at least a week while they went back to Havana to work. It was a time when Francisco felt entirely free. Expectations from his aunts and uncles were minimal: He was required to show up for meals, but if he forgot to wear shoes to the table, it was never mentioned. Having elbows on the table wasn't criticized, and running through the house was ignored. Not washing his hair every day was forgiven. But he knew adults were there and could be counted on if he needed them. The combination of freedom and security made for a special week in his life.

"Fishing!" Ramón said, leaping out of bed. "Let's get Tío Eduardo."

They caught up with their uncle on his way to the dock. Francisco was amazed that the tall man's long arms allowed him to carry a large cooler filled with ice, a five-gallon jug of water in one hand and a pail in the other. Wire fishing lines with hooks attached were draped around his neck. A cigarette — his favorite Competidora Gaditana ovalado — dangled from his lips, and another two packs were stuffed in the breast pockets of his shirt.

Directly overhead the sky was cloudless blue but a deep, heavy-looking gray hung over the ocean far out above the horizon to the north. A light breeze ruffled Francisco's hair. Waves were breaking in the distant deep-blue water, so the white foam looked like little lambs on their way home. He guessed that Tío Eduardo wouldn't take them out in these seas as far as he would like.

Francisco was wrong. His uncle gunned the 225 HP engine on the twenty-eight-foot boat and headed toward his favorite fishing spot. But when they reached it, waves tossed the boat about so much that the boys were forced to sink to their knees and hold the gunwale with one hand and a line with the other. After half an hour, Tío Eduardo turned the "Wima" back toward Matanzas Bay. In a quiet spot, they adjusted the weights near the ends of their cotton lines, jerked the knots holding the hooks to tighten them, and dropped them into turquoise-green water clear enough for Francisco to see bass biting both his and Ramón's lines at the same time.

Even so, the dark gray clouds moved closer. Eduardo called, "Pull them in, boys."

Francisco jerked, but his line wouldn't budge. He slipped overboard into the warm water, dove, and found his hook fastened to a coral reef. "Hey," he yelled, holding up a piece of the reef when he surfaced. "I caught Cuba!"

Tío Eduardo fileted the five bass on a rough wooden platform on the dock. The three fishermen took them to Humberto's kitchen where they watched as he dredged the fish in flour, fried them in deep oil, and placed them on three plates alongside baked sweet bananas and a mound of white rice with a fried egg on top.

When lunch was finished, Eduardo pulled a chaise to the spot directly under the overhead fan on the left side of the wrap-around porch — away from the afternoon sun — and stretched out for his siesta.

Saturday morning Francisco slept until 8:00 and then hung around the living room waiting for his parents to return before he left for a ride on his horse, Cacique. He sat down at the wooden game table in front of a jigsaw puzzle Tío Eduardo had brought. It was a snow scene from New York's Central Park. He laughed aloud and said to himself, "One thousand pieces of white."

When his mother's horn blared, Francisco jumped. Sprinting out the front door and down the steps, he saw his parents' car come to a stop and Tío Bernardo's mauve 1957 Bel Air Chevy stir up the dust as he passed and headed toward Tío Carlos's house. Carlos waved from the passenger's seat.

"That V8 can really move," he said, and then coughed.

"Why're you coughing? You all right?" His father got out of the passenger seat. Francisco nodded. "Help your mother unload the car. I have to change and get started on that pig."

By the time Francisco backed into the kitchen, his arms loaded with groceries, his father was wearing Humberto's long vinyl apron, holding a machete in one hand and a hammer in the other. He leaned over a medium-sized dead pig. The pig was on its back — legs and feet in the air — and Humberto was struggling to prevent it from rolling off the plastic tablecloth covering the wooden island in the middle of the room.

His father looked his way and muttered, "This is one big sucker." It had to be cut in two so the men could carry a half with each trip down the steps to the barbeque pit on the beach.

When Francisco saw his father stick the knife in the pig's neck, he swallowed and left the room.

At ten his father and uncles — Bernardo, Carlos, and Eduardo — made the two trips along the path and down the steps to the beach, carrying half the pig each time on the plastic cloth. Francisco and Ramón ran ahead carrying four folding chairs, a long-handled brush, and a bowl of mojo sauce to swab the pig before they covered it. From a distance the path they walked upon looked like pavement, but it was in truth made of shells that Francisco and Ramón had collected over the years. Most of the shells had broken when they had pressed them into the dirt, but once in a while Francisco would spot one that remained whole. The boys placed the chairs in a shallow cave behind the pit where the men could sit in the cool air out of the sun to watch over the pit.

When both halves of the pig had been swabbed with the sauce, buried in the charcoal Humberto had made, and covered, Francisco and Ramón sat down in the powdery white sand and watched heat rise from the pit. In the distance, Francisco noticed his father and uncles leaning forward in a huddle to whisper.

Francisco frowned. Somehow they looked different since they had returned from the city. He wondered if men could truly age that much in six days. His uncle Carlos was a large man in his sixties who had lost his right arm when a rifle exploded in a hunting accident. An ophthalmologist told him it was a miracle he hadn't lost his sight as well. In gratitude to God, he had said, he moved his internal medicine office from the upscale Miramar suburb to the old part of Havana, and treated many of the poor at no charge. Because of that he worked harder, but had been doing it for ten years or so.

Francisco couldn't believe what he saw: The last few days had had a pinched, aging effect on him.

His uncle Bernardo looked older, too. Having designed many buildings, including the National Library and the Maine Monument, he also was a hard worker, but being short and slim had always seemed to make him look younger until now.

Tío Eduardo was retired from his job at the National Institute of Health, but even though he hadn't gone to Havana the previous week, Francisco thought he looked as tired as the others.

His father was six feet tall and in good shape, but Francisco sensed that something was troubling him, too.

By the time the men and boys reached the kitchen, darkness was nearly complete. The pans they carried were filled with chunks of meat they had pulled from the roasted pig. Francisco's father banged against the door and groaned. Humberto jerked the door open, nearly causing him to fall. Francisco and Ramón grabbed the pan from their father's arms and rushed forward to set it on a counter. Francisco took a deep breath and sighed.

Humberto was cooking black beans, too. The lid was off the large aluminum pot and steam was drifting about. A breeze through the open shutters mingled with the scents Humberto had created, and filled the kitchen.

At 8:00, all the members of the Soler family on the farm — Tío Carlos and Tía Bet with three of their children; Tío Bernardo and Tía Raquel; Tío Eduardo and Tía Julia; Tías Elena and Juanita; and Francisco's mother and father with

Luisa, himself, and Ramón — all sixteen of them — gathered at a table meant for twelve. Someone had cut five wild yellow roses from the bushes by the front entrance and put them in a vase in the middle. Francisco held his breath as Humberto came in balancing two platters piled with pork surrounded by pieces of limes and two bowls of garlic and onion mojo sauce. He returned twice more for four bowls of rice, two of steaming black beans, and a platter of avocado and pineapple salad.

When the women and children began clearing empty plates from the table, Eduardo stood and raised his coffee cup. "Come on, Bernardo," he said to his brother-in-law. "Let's show these guys what real domino players can do."

"In your dreams!" Carlos roared as he pushed up from the table.

Pedro picked up the bag of dominoes and dumped all fifty-five tiles on the porch table, making a harsh cracking sound as they hit the smooth wooden surface.

While the men lit their cigars, Francisco and Ramón turned the tiles face down, shuffled them, and dealt each man ten. Smoke surrounded the table. Francisco sneezed.

Pedro touched Eduardo's shoulder. "You think you can take us, eh? Well, let's see what you've got." He picked up a tile from the fifteen set aside. "Well, well, well. Look at this." He grinned as he laid a double-nine tile in the middle of the table.

Ramón pulled a chair close to his uncle Eduardo, looked at his hand and whistled. Francisco glanced at his father's hand and then turned to watch the streaking flashes lightning bugs made across the black sky. Wonder what those insects have in mind, Francisco asked himself. There's no order to their flight that I can see. Just chaos, sort of like what's going on in Havana right now.

Monday afternoon, Francisco's cousins organized a softball game. Humberto's son, Bertito, gathered some of his friends to make the opposing team. Bertito pitched for both teams since all agreed that he had the best arm. A temperature of eighty-five and pink dust so thick they could barely see the bases shut the game down in half an hour and sent them racing to the beach until the sky turned yellow and the rumble of thunder and silver flashes of lightning sent them running for the house. Breathing hard, Francisco collapsed on the rough wood of the porch floor and watched water pour off the roof, splattering red dirt onto the side of the house.

Mid-morning Tuesday, Francisco and Ramón borrowed their cousin's twelve-foot boat to fish for bonito. Since it was late in the day for fishing, the boys didn't expect to catch much, so they let the little boat with its five-horsepower engine take them along as they drifted in and out of sleep. When Francisco awoke, he called to his brother, "Hey! We're in front of Morillo Castle at the river."

Protected by four cannons, Castillo del Morillo is a small fort built by the Spanish in 1720 to prevent pirates from entering the Canimar River.

Ramón got up on his knees and yelled, "Look!" pointing north toward the ocean. A school of sharks — each appearing to be two to three feet in diameter — were leaping out of the water and heading in a straight line toward their boat. Scrambling to get to Francisco, he dropped his new rod and reel in the water and screamed, "Get out of here!"

Francisco clutched the little skiff's tiller with trembling hands, held his breath, and headed straight for shore. Within minutes the sharks had disappeared, and the boys turned for home.

Late Friday, Silvia picked up Pedro from the bus station on the main road near the entrance to the farm. From his week in Havana, Pedro had brought six newspapers by different publishers. Before dinner, he and his brothers-in-law settled in wicker rockers under the left porch fan, each man with a daiquiri on a small metal table beside him, each grasping a creased newspaper. They read silently and sighed while Bernardo chewed on the end of an unlit cigar.

Francisco peeked over his father's shoulder and read. "July 23, 1959, President Urrutia Lleo was asked to resign and consented. Felt he could not work with the Marxists who have been placed in senior government and military positions. Fidel appoints Marxist Osvaldo Dorticós president, and continues to deny accusations that he's a communist."

Lower down on the front page, the story read: "Bishop expresses concern about communist government policies. Priests and lay church members imprisoned in work camps."

Dinner that evening was quiet. Pedro and Silvia ate quickly and left the table. Francisco wished he had a television to distract himself from his thoughts. The looks on his parents' faces troubled him. He lay down on top of the light blanket on his bed, and then got back up. The house was pitch-black, so holding onto the railing, he crept down the stairs. At the bottom, he stumbled over a chair someone had left where it didn't belong.

Even out on the porch, it was hot. The offshore breeze wasn't cool enough to make a difference. He sat down on a step and looked up. The sky held so many stars that almost none of it was black. That was as it should be, like a grayish-white lamp above him, but other things were not. What is happening? he wondered.

Saturday morning, Ramón leapt out of bed. "We didn't get up!" He shook Francisco. "Don't you remember? You said you'd go with me to watch the National Rowing Championships. I'm trying out next year and need some tips. Get moving!" Francisco groaned and rolled over.

August 14–21, 1959

*F*rancisco stood on the worn wooden platform at the train station in Matanzas, watching for the train. His godmother waited inside the station with their suitcases and tickets. The rest of the family had left Guaybaque for Havana, the summer almost over. Tía Elena had offered him an extra week of vacation, though, a visit to the cattle ranch owned by her first cousin, Anna. It was inland, near Cruces. Francisco's mother, his godmother, and Anna had been close friends since childhood. Anna was married to Tomás Cuervo, who had inherited the fifteen thousand-acre ranch where he raised prime beef.

When he finally saw the tracks vibrate and heard the whistle, Francisco turned and ran inside to pick up the suitcases.

The comfortable padded seats and the sway of the train car put his godmother to sleep soon after they started. She continued to doze throughout the four-hour trip. Francisco stared out the window. The wide expanses of grasses, large sugarcane fields, and hills in the distance held a beauty for him that Havana didn't have.

How innocent the cane fields look since the harvest, thought Francisco, only a few feet high. "They deceive you," he said aloud, thinking back to a conversation he had had with Humberto before dinner as he was watching him cook. Humberto described a friend's experience cutting cane. Although fully grown cane fields resemble green oceans with massive soft waves blown about by the wind, the ten-to-fifteen-foot-high leaves have razor sharp edges when mature, and snakes and rats run wild among the stalks. Cane cutters wear heavy, long-sleeved shirts, leather gloves, straw hats and boots, and use machetes to hack the thick, fibrous canes to a few inches above the ground before stacking them on their shoulders and loading them on truck beds, oxen carts or the trains that transport the cane to a mill for processing. Even though they have work for only four or five months a year during zafra — the harvest — and earn minimum wage, cane cutters know their work is respected because sugar brings more money to the country than any other export.

The train climbed as it neared the center of the island. Francisco took his handkerchief out of his back pocket and wiped the sweat from his face. Ocean breezes didn't reach this far inland.

Francisco had watched the barefoot children in loose pants and shirts playing outside bohios scattered along the track since they left Matanzas on their way to the larger city of Santa Clara. Most of the huts were made of wood, had an open frame for a window and a thatched grass roof. A few had metal roofs and some sides were patched with the same metal material. Clusters of banana palms were scattered about. I wonder what it's like living there, Francisco asked himself. No running water, no toilets. Schools? I read the government is building them, but then what? How do the children reach them without buses? The train passed three children running among several chickens and a goat. Clothes? He shook his head. So many problems. I hope Fidel's people know more than I do.

The train screeched and hissed as it slowed to a stop, then jerked forward. As he stood, Francisco saw cousin Anna on the platform waving her outstretched arm from side to side. Tía Elena knocked on the window and waved at her cousin.

Anna rushed up to them as they stepped off the train and gave prolonged hugs first to Elena and then to Francisco. Tomás' assistant, Manny, scooped up the suitcases with one arm and pointed toward the front of the building.

At six-foot-seven-inches, Manny was the tallest person Francisco had ever seen up close. Manny wore a cream-colored straw hat with one side folded up and a bandana over his hair tied at the back of his neck. The wide leather belt around his waist usually had a machete tucked under it on his left. His skin was shiny black.

When Manny opened the trunk of a 1957 Oldsmobile four-door sedan, Francisco let out a long whistle. "Hey, that's a Golden Rocket 88." He walked around the yellow and white two-tone beauty admiring the black top and the horizontal black racing stripe edged with chrome before slipping into the front seat beside Manny.

º"There he is," Francisco said as he pointed to one of his favorite people. Tomás sat in a rocking chair on the wide front veranda of the one-story wooden ranch house. He held a Cohiba cigar in one hand and a glass of rum in the other. His sun-streaked brown hair was in a long ponytail fastened at the back of his neck. When he rose to kiss his wife's cousins, he was quite round, weighing two-hundred-fifty pounds and standing five-feet-eight inches. The .38 Smith & Wesson six-shooter in the holster that dangled from his belt bumped Francisco's abdomen.

Manny disappeared inside the house with the suitcases and returned with a tray holding two glasses of sherry and a short glass of rum. Tomás dragged three more rockers across the porch and placed them close to his. Then he slapped Francisco on the back. "Big week planned for you!"

Tomás slept until noon every day. Francisco knew his routine, so he slept late himself. At 1:00 Manny led three saddled horses to the small porch off the back entrance to the house. Tomás stuffed his gray felt hat low on his head and handed a straw one to Francisco. Before getting on his horse, he strapped his Springfield rifle onto the back of Manny's saddle.

Led by Tomás with Manny bringing up the rear, the three rode across the pasture to the dairy. A few Jersey cows were huddled together in a fenced area under the feathery leaves of two massive tamarind trees.

Tomás slowed his horse to a walk and dropped back beside Francisco. "We're near what I want to show you. Got him from Texas right after your last visit here. I paid eight thousand dollars two years ago and got an offer this month from a guy in Camaguey to buy him for ten. Good deal, huh?"

Ahead Francisco saw an enormous animal — weighing nineteen hundred pounds, he would later be told — with large horns curving upward and a hump on his shoulders and neck. "That's a Brahman bull!" he shouted. "I've seen pictures of them."

After the three dismounted and tied their horses to a fence, Francisco wiped the dust from his nose and mouth.

"Smart boy," Tomás said while slapping him on the back. "He's manso, the perfect breeding animal for this climate. Heat doesn't bother him. That extra skin hanging around his throat and belly gives him more sweat glands and helps him cool off. His skin under that light gray hair is dark and bars the sunlight." Tomás laughed. "I call him Davy Crockett."

At four in the afternoon the day before his aunt and he were planning to leave, Francisco was lying on the bed in his room trying to keep cool with the overhead fan turned high. He had closed the window because of the dust. I'm ready for Havana's ocean breezes, he thought.

Tomás pounded on his door. "Come on. Something else to show you." Manny had pulled the car to the front steps.

It took thirty minutes to reach Santa Clara and another fifteen to find the cockfighting ring.

Cockfighting is one of the most popular sports in the country, and every city and village in Cuba has its cockfighting rings. In the old part of Havana and in some of the neighborhoods, too, large permanent structures have been built for frequent cockfights. In smaller towns, they are often improvised. In each location, though, gamecocks are bred for strength and endurance.

"You've never seen one of these, have you?" Tomás asked Francisco.

"No, Papy doesn't...."

"Of course not. Your father hasn't taken you to one even though there are probably a dozen or more rings in Havana. It's time for you to see one. Here's the way it goes. They shave the feathers of the cocks' chests and thighs and cut off the wattle. You know, that comb below the beak." Tomás went on to describe the curved metal spur, one to two-and-a-half inches long taped to the birds' legs above the natural spur. He said that in this area, the natural spur is sharpened instead of using the metal one. Roosters are paired according to body weight and fight to the death, unless one of the owners concedes and stops the fight. Rounds can last thirty minutes but most last much less time.

Just as Francisco, Tomás, and Manny reached the twelve-foot diameter ring, a double-sided wire cage hanging from a wooden frame ten feet above the ring was spun, the door latches pulled open by ropes. Two roosters, squawking and crying at once, their wings flapping, dropped to the ground. They landed in dirt, surrounded by concrete blocks built to a height of three feet and spattered with dried blood. The area stank of blood, feces, and urine. Heavy clouds of cigar smoke were another pungent layer drifting about the ring. Francisco's eyes watered at the smells. He hoped he wouldn't embarrass himself.

A man about Francisco's height with graying hair, weathered face, and wearing a loose, dirty muslin shirt, elbowed him and held out one peseta — twenty cents. He pointed to the red and black bird that had landed on its feet. "Mine, OK?"

"No. No." Francisco stepped back and shook his head.

Tomás grabbed Francisco's wrist, pressed a peseta into the palm of his hand and nodded, yes. "You've got the white one."

The white rooster leapt to its feet. Both birds lunged, wings flapping and beak-first, trying to pull feathers from the other's neck. When the white one turned, the red and black one slashed his belly and thigh, opening a two-inch gash. Blood spurted toward the men leaning over the wall. White rooster stepped back, raked his opponent's right eye with his left spur, and then quickly raked the left eye.

Francisco turned away and gagged.

Momentarily, red-and-black hesitated as if confused before charging his opponent with another slash to the body. The white rooster staggered and toppled over on his side.

Both owners jumped over the concrete wall, each picking up his rooster and holding him a few minutes while talking to the other man. Then they blew into their roosters' faces to annoy them, and dropped them into a smaller ring five feet in diameter.

The roosters struggled to their feet. Red-and-black

circled once, then twice. Francisco thought he might be blind. The white bird charged and slashed out three times. Red-and-black fell over, and lay still.

Tomás put his arm around Francisco's shoulders and smiled. The man in the muslin shirt handed him a peseta.

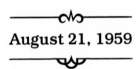

August 21, 1959

*F*rancisco climbed the hot stairwell of his home in Havana. He had been away for seven weeks. His hair had streaks of blond and his skin was nearly as dark as Arturo's. He had been sad, though relieved, to leave the farm. The adults had seemed preoccupied, so there hadn't been the usual amount of talk and laughter.

The Central Park puzzle had not been finished, its white sky still confused and undifferentiated. Even when Humberto and Tío Eduardo caught a ninety-pound wahoo, their excitement had been muted.

It will be good, Francisco thought, to get back to normal.

September 14, 1959

*F*rancisco mouthed, "Yes!" and slapped Arturo's shoulder when he read that his friend was in his class for their senior year. "Great, man," he said as the two of them walked down the noisy hall. "But we've got Brother David. Ugh. I've heard he'll give you a hard time if he doesn't like you."

When they neared the classroom door, Francisco stopped. "Why didn't you come to the farm this summer? You said you might."

Arturo shrugged. "I don't know."

Francisco stared at his friend. "But we were going fishing and you were going to help me with my fielding."

Arturo looked down the hall over Francisco's shoulder. "I looked for a job." He lowered his voice. "The hotel isn't giving Mami enough work: too empty. She only has twenty hours now." He bit his lower lip. "I couldn't find one."

When the boys entered the classroom, Brother David was writing on the chalkboard. He stepped aside and read aloud: "No one is allowed to talk about the government or the revolution in this school. Read the newspapers." He had underlined every word.

A fly buzzed Francisco's left ear. He brushed it away but it returned, dive-bombing into the damp stickiness of his other ear.

"Another announcement," Brother David continued. "There will be no more charges to anyone for books or writing materials." He sighed heavily. "Surely, though, you all must know that one-third of our students in our three Havana schools are already on a scholarship, and in Santiago de Cuba, Christian Brother schools are free for all students. I'm not sure..." He shook his head. The tall, thin man leaned forward, the white ties that draped from his stiff collar dangling as he jabbed his right index finger toward his thirty-four students. "It is vitally important to your future that you do well in this, your last, year at De La Salle."

September 15, 1959

$\mathcal{F}$rancisco read the headlines of *La Marina* first thing because his father had put it beside his plate the following morning. "Government continues land seizures!" the headline shrieked.

That afternoon he waited on the sidewalk in the shade of a flamboyant tree for his mother to pick him up after baseball practice. He leaned hard against the trunk of the umbrella-shaped tree, causing a few of its orange-gold blossoms to fall on his shoulders just as his mother pulled up beside the curb in front of his school.

"Abuela told me at lunch you had decided to pick me up today. Why, Mami? Are we going somewhere?"

"No, hijo." She shook her head. "Oh, I don't know. I just wanted to make sure you got home all right." She turned off the car engine, and laid her hand on Francisco's shoulder. "And I have something to tell you."

"What?" Francisco started to remind her he was old enough to get home on his own, but hesitated when he saw the sad look on her face. "Mami, what land is the government taking?"

Tears came to Silvia's eyes and her voice cracked. "They've confiscated — stolen — Tomás' ranch — Anna's!"

She inhaled and exhaled loudly. "Anna said the militia showed up two days ago and told them to leave. Said bonds would be mailed to them in compensation. Those low-interest bonds paid out over many years. Good luck, I say. Nobody has received any of them. Tomás' brothers left for Spain in May, but he stayed because he felt responsible for the cattle." Tears slowly filled the creases in her cheeks. "Now they'll have to leave, too."

Francisco didn't like seeing his strong, confident mother so anxious. He wanted to change the subject but was drawn to it. "Where are Anna and Tomás now?"

"They both came to Havana. The government wants to run all the businesses, but," she seemed to have trouble speaking for a moment, "they're stupid! They killed his best bull! Tomás was trying to explain how to take care of the Brahman because it was used for breeding and was so valuable — worth ten thousand pesos — when the officer in charge took out his pistol and shot it in the head. 'We don't have to do all that,' he said, 'we'll just eat ten one-thousand-peso steaks.' Then, he — he laughed." Tears streamed down her face. "Tomás was so proud of that bull."

October 1959

*M*onday night, Francisco set the alarm for six-thirty to give himself half an hour to read the newspaper before leaving for school. He wanted to understand what was going on in his country. He suspected that his parents, aunts, and uncles discussed it often since they had started gathering in Tía Elena's living room every day before dinner. Each time he had tried to slip in without being noticed, they stopped talking.

Pedro held a cup of café con leche in one hand and a croissant in the other. *La Marina* was spread out on the table before him. He looked up when Francisco entered the dining room. "What are you doing up so early?" his father asked when Francisco sat down already dressed in his school uniform.

Francisco pointed to the newspaper. "I want to read what you've finished."

His father shook his head. "Not sure that's a good idea. Confusing." But he pushed the front section toward him.

The first half of the front page described the four new water and sanitation projects intended for the eastern half of the island; the planners had finished the design stage and would start building immediately. Blocks of apartments, housing seven hundred families, had been completed in two rural provinces. Each held a day-care center that was free to all who lived there. More workers were needed to staff these centers and people were encouraged to leave the cities to help. The government had sent teachers and health-care workers to ten rural communities to open schools and clinics. The goal was for all Cubans to have basic skills in reading and arithmetic through the sixth-grade level and to have instruction in good revolutionary citizenship. Classes were also being opened in factories to teach reading and writing.

Francisco smiled. Great, he thought, this is good. Wonder why Papy's confused? Turning the page, he noticed the name Camaguey. The article stated that a group of wealthy cattlemen whose ranches were being confiscated had joined forces and had appealed to Major Huber Matos, the military governor of the province, and to the anti-communist wing of Fidel's original revolutionary group, the 26th of July Movement.

The article described how former rural school-teacher and small rice farmer, Huber Matos, joined the urban underground to oppose Batista's dictatorship. He won the friendship of Fidel Castro and became a valuable officer in his group when he smuggled weapons, medicine, and fighters into Cuba from Costa Rica at a time when Fidel's forces in the Sierra Maestra Mountains were badly in need of support. A well-respected and courageous man, he — along with a number of other officers — believed in revolution but was adamantly opposed to the communist policies and practices infiltrating the new government. He declared himself in favor of free enterprise as well as improvement in the standard of living for the rural poor.

Also good, thought Francisco. I agree with him. Wonder if they'll give the land back.

Sunday morning, Francisco awoke to the rattle of his shutters as heavy rain pelted them. The hurricane's here, he thought, groaning.

Francisco pulled up the hood of his poncho when his mother stopped the car at the corner of D and Thirteenth Streets. While running past the line of cars, he wondered if the buses were operating, and whether Arturo would be given a penalty for not attending mass if they weren't. It surprised him that he had never asked his friend a question like that.

The wind and rain continued through Sunday afternoon. Francisco's parents were at Tía Elena's and Luisa was lying on the couch reading. When he sat down in his father's chair, he noticed a newspaper that had been rolled up and stuffed between the cushion and the inside of the chair. He took the paper to the dining table and spread it out to look for anything that might catch his attention. When he spotted the name Huber Matos at the bottom of page one, he read, "The former Major Matos was arrested at his home in

Las Villas and brought to Havana in chains. He was taken to La Cabaña prison and will be tried for his crimes — counter-revolutionary offenses."

What? Francisco thought. How can Fidel arrest his friend? He read every word of the remaining pages. On Page Four he saw, "KGB agent seen in Cuba. East German Stasi secret police training members of Cuban Intelligence Service, G2." Secret police force? They're creating another one? Why?

November 1959

*F*rancisco, Luisa, and their mother sat at their places at the dinner table. Rosa pushed the kitchen door partly open and looked in. Silvia shook her head, no. Rosa closed the door.

"Where is he, Mami? Where's Papy?" Luisa asked.

Silvia turned first to her son and then to Luisa, a look of surprise on her face. "Well, dear, I have to say I don't know. Can you remember a time when he was late for dinner?"

Pedro opened the front door and called, "Sorry. Tell Rosa to serve." Then he roughly pulled back his dining chair and sat down.

"Dear," Silvia said as she placed her hand on his, "something must be wrong."

"They want an audit!" he said. "Can you believe that? Some jackass ordered it from that new layer of government bureaucracy they've piled on. We just did one in March like the same one we've done every year for the last eleven since the hospital opened." Pedro lightly slapped the slick plastic placemat with his palm and turned to his right to face his wife. "They'll start with hospital equipment, then move through it all. Pharmacy, too."

"What a waste of time," Silvia said. "What will come of it? And why are they doing it again?"

"Probably just a show of power." He took a deep breath. "It'll cause a headache, but it'll pass."

When Rosa set a large platter of chicken in front of Pedro, he looked up. "Thank you. This will make me feel better."

Francisco's mouth watered as he watched his father spoon the garlic cloves, onions, and lime sauce over his chicken and rice. Two others would fill their plates before it was his turn. "Leave me some sauce," he requested.

Silvia smiled, patted her son's arm and turned back to her husband. "Who's in charge?"

"I put Victor on it. He's become mostly worthless. Nobody wants him in their operating room anymore — even to assist." He shook his head. "Something about the guy...."

"Isn't he the one who was shot, Papy?" Luisa asked.

Pedro grinned.

"Not many surgeons in Cuba — or anywhere in the world — have been shot at their workplace by a patient's brother."

"But didn't the patient die?"

"Well, yes, it's a tragic story. And it shouldn't have happened. It was just incompetence on Victor's part. He never should have been an orthopedic surgeon."

"And you saved his life," Luisa continued.

Her father nodded. "That's right. Lucky he was in the hospital when it happened. After that, the board reviewed Victor's work and wouldn't let him operate alone anymore. Just tragic all the way around."

Francisco waited fifteen minutes for his mother beside the crimson bougainvillea on the front wall bordering the tennis club before giving up and walking to the bus stop. She had been picking him up most days and this would have been a good day to have a ride because his head was hurting from his collision with Roberto at football practice. Each step caused his head to throb more.

Finally, he thought, as he unlocked the front door.

When he opened the living-room door, his mother and father were in their chairs and Luisa was sitting instead of lying on the couch. His mother's face was red. One of the combs that held the hair back from her forehead was missing, allowing a few curls to drape over. She pushed them aside and said, "Oh, hijo, I forgot!"

"Sit down, Francisco. I have something to say." His father's voice was harsh. "I'm no longer director of the National Orthopedic Hospital. I was fired today by the new government health minister."

"What?" Luisa's eyes widened. "But why?"

Pedro rubbed his neck before answering. "Who really knows? But the official reason given is that I *stole* a wall urinal. They finished the so-called audit in four days and found one missing. I'm being held responsible. A less official reason is that I accepted an award from Batista — therefore, I'm a counter-revolutionary."

Silvia covered her eyes with her right hand and let out a sob.

"But that was your award from the Medical Society." Luisa said.

Pedro nodded. "Yes, for my work with polio victims. But since it was the dictator who handed it to me, they think I must have been his crony." He stood quickly. "What a farce! My office was cleared out this morning, and Victor moved in. The most incompetent physician in the hospital was made director."

Exactly one week later, Silvia received a letter from the director of the hospital pharmacy telling her she was no longer needed in her position as his assistant. Francisco watched as his mother first screamed, then cried. He was sorry for her and his father, but he didn't know how to react. No one he trusted seemed in control of life anymore and all he knew to do was to look over his shoulder more often. To watch, listen, and hide.

Francisco awoke after a restless sleep. His pajamas were wet with sweat. He looked at the window and found the shutters closed tightly, but didn't remember doing that. He turned toward the clock and saw that it was 6:00. Good, he thought. I'll get the paper and read it before Papy gets up. He dressed quickly in his school uniform and headed down the hall. When he reached the living room, he heard, "Where are you going?"

Startled by his father's voice so early in the morning, Francisco spun around. "What?"

Although his father no longer had to be at work until 3:00 in the afternoon for his private patients downstairs, he was sitting in his chair in the living room. *La Marina* was divided into three sections, two folded and tucked on each side of him, one open on his lap. "Why are you up so early?" Pedro asked.

"Couldn't sleep." Francisco pointed to the newspaper. "And wanted to do what you're doing."

His father motioned toward the couch. "Sit down, hijo."

Francisco sat heavily. "I can wait," he said.

"What's on your mind?"

"Don't know." Francisco shook his head. "Well, Papy." He looked at his father. "I wonder what's going to happen. From one day to the next, things change."

Pedro rolled up the front section of the paper and tossed it to his son. "You're right, a lot of change. It's not finished, but what you'll read in there will help move things along. People aren't satisfied and are resisting. Powerful people, so this can't go on much longer. Somebody else from the army will step up and stop these communists — or the U.S. will. Soon. Turn to the next-to-the-last page."

Two letters to the editor — one from Mrs. Huber Matos and another from Major Huber Matos — were printed side by side. Señora Matos complained of her husband's treatment in prison. After all his sacrifices to bring about the revolution, she said he was now being tortured for speaking his own mind and was being held in a three-by-ten-foot cell with little food and few clothes.

Major Matos' letter accused Fidel Castro of betraying the Cuban people. He said he had proof that a communist dictatorship was the government's goal and that he had shown his evidence to Camilio Cienfuegos before his plane had disappeared. Cienfuegos would have resisted this betrayal with every ounce of his being, Matos wrote. He concluded that the intention of the revolution had never been to establish a communist government but was, instead, to bring about democracy and an economy that brought the rural poor into the mainstream of Cuban life.

Francisco laid down the paper. "Papy, what do they think happened to Cienfuegos' plane?"

"Son, you know you must not ask questions like that outside this house, don't you?"

Francisco nodded.

"People think Fidel had him killed."

"But why would he?" Francisco asked. "They were good friends and fought together from the beginning. People liked him."

Pedro slapped the newspaper. "Exactly. His popularity rivaled Fidel's. And he was not a communist. People respected him so much they might have turned against Fidel if he asked them to. And he was Huber Matos' friend. He may have gone against Fidel in that arrest. Too risky for Fidel: our great leader tolerates no dissent and crushes all competitors."

Wow, Francisco thought. Why didn't I get that?

At the bottom of the front page, Francisco read, "The First National Catholic Congress will be held today at 7:00 p.m. in the Plaza of the Revolution — at the José Martí Monument — to protest actions of the government."

Francisco handed the paper back to his father. "So it'll soon be over?"

Pedro nodded. "Not too long, I imagine."

When his mother dropped him off at school, Francisco waited until he was on the sidewalk before calling out, "I'll be late for dinner. Save it for me." Then he slammed the car door.

As soon as football practice was over, Francisco ran out the door of the club and down Calzada to Paseo where thirty to forty people milled about on the corner. He elbowed past ten or so until a man grabbed his shoulder and said, "Wait." Then he slipped under a low-hanging queen-palm frond and leaned against the trunk of the tree, suddenly aware of his growling stomach. The screeching and grinding of brakes returned his attention to his mission. A bus slowed before speeding up without stopping. People around him groaned. Some muttered, "Too full." A man nearby turned on a transistor radio and filled the air with bolero music. A woman standing beside Francisco snapped her fingers, swayed her hips, and winked at him. He grinned and looked at his watch — 6:30. Three more buses passed before an empty one stopped, and the crowd that had increased to nearly fifty pushed those in front of them up the steps.

Francisco couldn't see the stage at the plaza so he focused on the people around him as he listened to the bishop's message from a speaker attached to a lamppost above his head. Most looked like they had just come from work in offices, department stores, hotels, and homes. There were nuns dressed in black and white habits alongside mothers holding the hands of their young children. He wondered what was different from the time Fidel entered nearly a year ago. Oh, yeah, he thought. No soldiers and no people from the countryside are here.

The bishop's words came through clearly. "In the new schools, my brothers, our children are being taught there is no God. Priests and laypersons of the Church are being imprisoned for speaking out against immoral acts. Catholic citizens are prevented from participating in new development projects. Thousands of our fellow Cubans are being beaten, starved, and worked to death in detention centers for opposing the government. We do not want communism! Let your voices be heard!"

Many people around Francisco crossed themselves and cheered as they surged forward toward the platform. Francisco noticed that the street-lights had come on, and the sky was graying. He glanced at his watch, 8:00, and knew his mother would be worried, so he turned in the opposite direction, dodging and pushing when necessary. When finally free from the crowd, he ran the ten blocks to Twenty-third Street where he waited for a bus. Maybe this will make the difference Papy has talked about, he thought. Yes. Yes.

The next morning Francisco saw the headlines of *La Marina*: "One million people attend anti-communist rally!"

Silvia set the plate of bread in front of him. "I'll pick you up at the club after school."

"I'm staying at school for baseball."

"But baseball season is over. There's no practice."

Francisco held up a piece of bread. "Mami, it's not toasted."

Silvia flipped her right hand at her son. "Hijo, eat! Rosa's busy and I'm in a hurry. I have to get you there on time, and then drop Luisa at the university. Too much. Too much." She frowned and waved her arms. "Just be ready in five minutes."

"Why doesn't Papy learn to drive?" he whispered.

Francisco didn't want to tell his mother that he was staying at school because Arturo wanted to practice hitting and needed a pitcher, even a bad one. He was afraid she would insist he go to the club, and he didn't want to explain his concern for Arturo. Something about him had changed in the past two months. He was quieter, rarely smiled, and practiced baseball every available minute. He was keeping up with his schoolwork because every Monday morning, when names were called to line up according to weekly grades, he took his usual place as number five, but Francisco was still worried about his friend.

The petals of a bougainvillea vine littered the sidewalk beside the front entrance to the school where Francisco waited for his mother. Although Silvia slowed, she didn't bring the car to a complete stop, so Francisco held onto the doorframe and swung himself in, pretending his moll was picking him up after a bank robbery.

"I'm getting you first so you can go in and find Luisa if she's not out front," Silvia said.

Francisco sighed when his mother stepped on the break at the front entrance of the two-story white-stucco University of Havana main building. No Luisa.

"Where do I go?" he asked.

"Ask for the humanities building or the library."

As Francisco ran up the wide steps and past the eight marble columns lining the front of the central courtyard, he wondered if he would ever be climbing these as a student. When the university had reopened in September, Luisa had enrolled as a freshman but complained that, after a month's time, the registrar still didn't have her high-school transcript. When asked how things were going, she usually shook her head and said, "I'm not sure." He found her sitting on a cement bench in the courtyard with a large stack of books beside her — her head shaded by the fronds of a king palm.

Luisa rose and picked up the books when she saw him.

"Why weren't you waiting on the sidewalk?" he asked.

She shrugged. "Umm, I don't know. Just didn't feel comfortable out there."

At home Francisco ran ahead of his mother and sister, turned on the TV, and stretched out on the couch. Fidel Castro's face filled the screen on all three channels. "Do not let your guard down, my brothers and sisters! We are still fighting for the revolution. There are those among you who would undo all we have accomplished — the schools, the new houses, the clinics, the equalization of land holdings, the breaking up of great wealth, the new roads, new dignity, pride, independence from those who would patronize us.

"Beware, my friends, they want to turn us back to the past. We are stopping them but need your help. Watch and listen! Report what you hear! You are the eyes and ears of the revolution!" Francisco stood and turned off the TV. Good grief, he thought. You sound like a crazy man.

That night, Francisco had trouble sleeping, so he went back to the living room and turned on the TV again. Fidel's face was still there, his words continuing like a hammer beating against Francisco's skull.

December 1959

*F*rancisco's father stared at the ropa vieja on his plate and flicked out the slices of green bell pepper with his fork. He stirred the flank steak around, mixing it with the rice and black beans even though he had never liked for one food to touch another until they reached his mouth.

Francisco watched as Luisa turned first to her mother and then to her father before pushing her chair back from the dining table and going to the record player. She flipped through the pile of seventy-eights, chose a Benny Moré album, and turned it on loud enough so that none of them could hear even if they had wanted to talk. Her father didn't look up from his plate but her mother nodded. Rosa — a surprised look on her face — cracked open the kitchen door and peeked in.

They're not themselves, Francisco thought. I need to talk to Madrina.

Pedro left the table first, not waiting for dessert. Then Silvia and Luisa drifted away one by one. Francisco went to his room, picked up his logic and history of Latin America books and pushed on the heavy mahogany door that led from his bedroom to the stairway. At the bottom of the stairs he heard Tía Julia's shrill voice and leaned on his godmother's living room door for a moment before opening it. "And she had the nerve to tell me I was being unfair and I should share what I have." Francisco pressed his ear against the door, and gently stacked his books on the floor. His aunt continued. "I had to fire her! Having a cook who supports the communists is too risky. She could report us for some comment or just make up something if she gets mad. Too dangerous. I told her finances were uncertain and we couldn't afford her." She hesitated. "And it's true. Eduardo's bank account is still frozen. We may never see that money again."

More was said but Julia had lowered her voice, so Francisco couldn't make it out. Tía Juanita said something that he couldn't understand either. His body drifted onto the floor beside his books. When he saw his hands shaking, he stood quickly and pushed open the door, leaving the books in the stairwell. He strode into the room with his usual broad smile, going directly to his godmother and kissing her on her nose. She nearly pulled him off his feet onto her lap but he held back.

"I'm sorry I'm late," he said.

"Mi Panchito, where are your books?"

Besides his aunts, Tío Eduardo sat in the living room, filling it with his cigarette smoke. Eduardo glanced at Francisco before slowly getting up from the large wing chair and walking toward the balcony. He swung open the two French doors. Francisco felt a cool breeze rush in along with the horns from the street and cha-cha music from the apartment upstairs.

Eduardo turned to face his wife, his two sisters-in-law, and Francisco. "I'm a Cuban. I know and trust my people. We fought for and won our independence in 1902 from a country that once was one of the most powerful in the world. When I was in my thirties, there was the dictator Machado's secret police force that arrested anyone — artists, journalists, professionals — he didn't like. Many disappeared. We had poverty and corruption. Many fled the country." He looked at his wife. "We lived in New Orleans for years because of his terror." Eduardo paused to light another cigarette. "But we're here and they're not. This too will pass."

Elena pulled Francisco into the chair beside her. She had one arm behind him and the other across his chest. He felt himself shaking. "Try not to worry, my son," she said.

After school the next day, Francisco waited at the bus stop on the corner of Calzada and Paseo. Warm air swirled about him in great gusts. A hurricane was coming. It crossed his mind that his mother would be worried if he wasn't on the corner at the club when she came to pick him up, but he dismissed that thought when a question came to him: Who could take care of anyone these days, anyway? Arturo hadn't come to school that morning and he intended to find out why. It wasn't just that he hadn't come to school, though Francisco couldn't think of another day he had missed, but he hadn't been himself for months and only one person could tell him what was wrong with his friend.

Just as the long gray bus came to a halt, the vendor at the sidewalk coffee stand rang the bell signaling that a fresh pot of coffee was ready. The bus driver opened the front door and jumped out. While he drank his shot-glass-sized cup, Francisco pushed his way on with the crowd and stood in a back corner beside a young boy sucking on a piece of sugarcane.

The street where Arturo lived was nearly empty of people though Francisco did hear merengue music coming from an open doorway and saw a dozen or so men gathered there. He tried to remember where the whorehouse was. He shrugged. Government had banned prostitution. Too bad. Really none of their business, he thought.

Francisco was beginning to doubt his sense of direction when at last he recognized the large arched wooden door edged with metal studs. He looked up. There was the blue wooden balcony. Not seeing a doorbell, he began knocking.

"They're gone," a woman said from behind him.

Francisco spun around to face a black woman. "No. I'm looking for Señora López and Arturo. He goes to my school."

The elderly woman turned her back to the wind and pulled her shiny orange and green shawl across her chest. "They moved in with your friend's aunt. Señora López's sister. Near the train station."

Francisco looked at his watch and shook his head. The train station is too far to go there now. If I try, I'll never make it home by dinner, he thought.

As the bus traveled along the Malecón beside the roiling sea, Francisco watched as tops of royal palms were flung into each other by the strong winds. Ordinarily, the enormous dark clouds and wild winds that hurricanes brought excited him. Today, they did not. Just what we need, he thought. More upheaval.

The next morning when Silvia backed the car out of the driveway, she stopped in front of Bernardo's building to avoid the flooded street in front of her own. The hurricane had turned out to be a tropical storm, cleaning the buildings and streets with its rain and leaving a bright blue cloudless sky. Francisco slipped into the back seat behind his mother and sister.

"I should have told you last night, Mami, they're cancelling my Spanish literature class," Luisa said. "They say they don't know where Señor Aguilera is." Luisa lowered her voice as if she was about to whisper before raising it again. "I heard from Mari that he may have been arrested."

"Dear, why didn't you tell us?"

Luisa looked out the window, away from her mother. "I didn't want to talk about it. What's the point? What can we do? And, actually, that's nothing. I may not get credit for any of my classes because they *say* they still haven't received my high-school transcript. Poo! They probably lost it."

Francisco didn't want to hear about his sister's problems with classes; he just wanted to get to school to see if Arturo was there.

He ran from the car to the front doors and stopped before surveying the hallway. Uh-oh, he thought. Halfway down stood the teacher with the nickname, el policia, because of his unforgiving eagle-eye. Francisco slowed, each step deliberate until he reached his classroom door and he saw Arturo in his usual seat.

Francisco punched his buddy on the upper arm. "Man, where were you yesterday?"

Arturo kept his eyes on his desk. "Tell you later."

Francisco would have to hurry to make it to his grandmother's house for lunch on time, but he waited at the end of the hall for Arturo anyway. His friend walked slowly.

"Man, what happened?" Francisco asked.

Arturo shook his head. "We had to move. Mami's brother brought his car over and I stayed to help them."

"Where did you go?" Francisco asked.

"Moved in with Tía Lupe, Mami's sister. She lives near the train station."

"But," Francisco wrinkled his brow, "you lived in a good place." He followed his friend outside.

Arturo motioned for them to step out of the crowd and lowered his voice. "Mami can't find work. Tía Lupe has a job cleaning some of the university buildings." He looked up at the sky. "You hear the government telling us all the time that we don't need so much and we should share. Do with less." He looked back at Francisco. "Well, think maybe they'll call me a good citizen now that I sleep on the couch?" He shook his head. "Just forget it. Can you pitch for me after school?"

"You think the field will be dry enough?" Francisco asked.

"Got to anyway. They'll be sending scouts down soon, and I have to be ready."

December 1959

A headline at the bottom of *La Marina*'s first page caught Francisco's eye. "Huber Matos' trial begins today." He glanced at the date: December 11.

"Did you see this, Papy? Major Matos is going to trial."

"Yes. Hard to believe his arrest didn't stir up some opposition in the military and, maybe, arouse the U.S. But, no. No one has any guts these days."

The following morning, *La Marina* described the first day of the Matos trial. "Huber Matos' trial was held in an army movie theater before a crowd of one thousand five hundred soldiers and members of the international press. The chief prosecution witness was the man he had aided when in need — Fidel Castro. Fidel spoke to the court for seven hours, claiming Matos was working with the Americans, the

CIA, and wealthy cattle-ranchers to thwart the revolution's goals."

Four days after the Matos trial began, Francisco read, "Huber Matos, the man who fought so bravely for his country, sentenced to twenty years in prison."

The next day after school Francisco decided to go back to his usual routine of taking the bus to the club after school and waiting on the steps right at 7:00 for his mother to pick him up. I'll show some guts by living normally again, he thought.

At 4:45, when he rounded the corner to the tennis club, he saw six bearded young men wearing olive-green military fatigues standing at the bottom of the front steps. They stood facing each other, leaving space just wide enough for one person at a time to go up the marble steps and into the building. He stopped beside the bougainvillea and then stepped behind it.

Should I go in, or turn around and take the bus home? he wondered. Mami would tell me to go home, but, no, I'm getting back to my life. He wiped his sticky palms on his trousers, slung his book bag over his shoulder, and approached the soldiers. One whispered something to another beside him and switched his rifle from one hand to the other. Francisco kept his gaze focused on the open doors ahead and climbed the eight steps.

Four men about his father's age dressed in long-sleeved navy shirts and pants were talking to each other in an otherwise empty foyer. They stopped and stared at him when he entered. One muttered, "marqueses," and the others snickered. Francisco flushed. He knew they were making fun of the "marqués" nickname that members of other clubs had given tennis club members, suggesting they were arrogant and thought of themselves as rich Spanish noblemen. That puzzled him since the wealthy in Cuba generally weren't members of their club. They belonged to Havana Yacht Club, Havana Biltmore Yacht Club, and the Havana Country Club.

He held his breath, trying to make himself invisible, as he moved slowly through the trophy room and into his locker room. When Francisco tossed his bag toward a bench, it landed upright and on top. That made him smile briefly before turning around. Standing in front of a locker and tucking a T-shirt into the waistband of his shorts was el gago. Francisco groaned silently. He needed to know what was going on but the only person he could ask stuttered so much that he accepted his nickname without complaint.

Francisco sat down on a bench in front of el gago and pulled his shirt and shorts from his bag. "What's happening?" he asked, then forced himself to listen to the repetitious sounds without interrupting or correcting.

He learned that a member of the club, Señor Gutiérrez, had been arrested that morning when he arrived for work at his insurance office and was charged with counter-revolutionary activities. His accuser was his own son, Armando. Undercover police had come to the club to interview people who knew the elder Gutiérrez.

Once more Francisco asked himself if he should get dressed and go home. Again he heard his mother's voice: "Of course, you should!" But he decided against it. He wanted to know more. When he left the locker room, el gago was still there. Keeping his head down, Francisco slipped away from the men in dark clothing and rounded the corner on his way to the handball court. Boys his age could hang out there without being bothered by adults.

He pictured Señor Gutiérrez — a large, exceptional athlete with a head of thick black hair who wore a white guayabera shirt, summer and winter. Francisco liked him, but not his son. Because it was widely known that Armando used drugs, most kids at the club wouldn't hang out with him. When he was expelled from De La Salle High School, his father forced him to enroll in Havana Military Academy.

When Francisco pulled on the squeaky door of the hand-ball court, he was taken aback by the strong smell of sweat. A group of ten boys squatted on the shiny wooden floor. Three of them — fear on their faces — jumped up before they saw who he was. Roberto signaled for him to join them. Francisco listened as they repeated what el gago had already told him, before adding that each man at the club was being taken into a room alone and asked what he had heard Señor Gutiérrez say about the government. Then they started over, wondering aloud if anyone knew where Armando was.

Francisco tapped Roberto on the shoulder, pointed to the clock near the ceiling, and rose slowly. Roberto followed. As they crossed the patio by the pool and approached the outdoor bar, the men standing there fell silent.

Francisco grabbed his school clothes from his locker, stuffed them in his duffel bag, and, keeping his eyes straight ahead, ran down the front steps and turned the corner to Twelfth Street. He wanted to meet his mother before she saw the soldiers.

Those damn barbudos. How I hate beards now, he thought. He waited under a mango tree until he spotted the dark-blue Chrysler inching its way toward him. He stepped off the curb, waved, and grabbed the door handle.

"Hijo," his mother said, "that's dangerous. Why are you on the street?"

"In a hurry to get home." He laid his hand on his mother's arm and smiled broadly, trying to charm her out of anger. "A lot of homework tonight."

"Francisco, Isabel wants to talk to you." Luisa grinned as she held up the phone.

"I don't know who Isabel is. Leave me alone." Francisco turned to walk away.

His sister covered the phone's mouthpiece with her hand. "Come here! She's in my class at school. You remember her from Carnaval. I told her you would go to her party."

Francisco stepped back. "But why me? I'm not in your class, and you're all older!"

Luisa's voice softened. "Oh, come on. Help us out. We want to have a party and a lot of the boys our age have left. She'll invite Roberto, too."

When Friday came Francisco considered saying he was sick so he wouldn't have to go to Isabel's party because he was certain he wouldn't know anyone there except Luisa and Roberto. He had agreed to go only because Luisa begged him, and then stood beside him while he was on the phone, pinching his upper arm and mouthing, "Yes."

But he had another reason for giving in. Isabel lived near the country club, and he had heard that a house in that neighborhood had been taken by Fidel when he left the Hilton Hotel. Its wealthy owners had left the country. Francisco didn't know the name or address but assumed it would be easy to find because of the large number of soldiers attending Fidel. He knew he wouldn't be able to get close but thought he could at least see something.

His plan was to slip away from the party with Roberto after dinner. If Roberto asked why he wanted to do that, he wasn't sure he could explain it. All he knew was that this leader's actions confused and angered him. He condemned the rich. OK, he thought, I can understand that, but why would he want to live in one of their houses in the most expensive neighborhood in Havana?

Luisa waved goodbye when her mother stopped the car at 9:30 in front of a two-story modern house. Francisco remained in the car. "Mami, look at that." He pointed to a curved roof with the front raised as if it were reaching for the stars.

This is change I like, he thought. New. Interesting. Exciting. He had seen these houses but hadn't been in one. Now he was glad he came.

"Wait, Mami, don't go until Roberto gets here." Just as he finished, Roberto's father roared up the circular drive in his blue-and-white Mercury convertible with the top down.

Before the boys could reach for the doorbell, a servant dressed in a white dinner jacket and black pants opened the door, greeting them, "Buenas noches." A man in a navy blue suit and a woman in a long black dress waited in the foyer. When Isabel's mother turned to greet Francisco, her waist-length double strand of pearls brushed against his hand.

The servant directed the boys to an interior patio where Isabel, Luisa, and four other girls and boys stood beside a twelve-foot Christmas tree. Francisco had guessed correctly. He didn't know anyone here. A waiter interrupted his thoughts by presenting a tray of crystal glasses filled with rum and Coke, lemonade, and Spanish cider. Francisco and Roberto each chose a rum and Coke.

Isabel's parents sat in large overstuffed chairs along a wall of the octagonal patio, a small table holding glasses of sherry between them. Pots of four-foot-tall white orchids were to their right and left. They talked with each other while occasionally glancing up and smiling at their daughter's friends.

The young people were soon summoned to a lace-covered dining table appointed with two large silver candelabra and silver vases filled with soft green hydrangeas. Francisco was seated between two girls he hadn't yet spoken to and across the wide table from Roberto. A waiter filled their champagne glasses with the same Spanish cider — a picture of a Spaniard playing a bagpipe on the label — that his parents sometimes drank.

Francisco took a small bite of the lobster thermidor served in its tail shell. Umm, he thought, this is almost as good as the one Humberto makes. He sneaked glances at the girls to his left and to his right. They're cute, he thought, but what else can I say to girls I don't even know? I've already told them four jokes.

At that moment a waiter placed a small crystal fingerbowl beside each plate. Francisco watched as Roberto picked up his bowl, brought it toward his mouth, and used his finger to push aside the pansy that floated on top. He tried to kick his friend to warn him, but the table was too wide. Francisco's jaw dropped. As Roberto drank the water, Francisco held his sides and laughed until tears came to his eyes.

When the pineapple cake was finished, they were escorted to the patio beside the pool. Strands of white lights stretched along wide umbrella-like limbs of the flamboyant trees. Isabel's parents now sat at a small round table where cups of espresso had been placed on a white embroidered cloth.

Isabel lifted the needle of the record player and dropped it just as the girl who had sat to Francisco's left at dinner grabbed his hand and pulled him forward, causing him to forget Fidel Castro even existed.

December 24, 1959

$\mathcal{F}$rancisco leaned against the kitchen door inhaling the scents of roasting pork and frying plantains. It was Noche Buena, and Tío Eduardo and Tías Julia, Elena, and Juanita had come to celebrate Christmas Eve with his family. Pedro shoved open the sliding glass door, and he and Eduardo stepped inside from the balcony. A strong north wind pushed Tío Eduardo's cigarette smoke ahead of them and into the living room.

"Pedro!" Francisco's mother turned toward her husband. "The wind will ruin the table." Francisco's father handed her his daiquiri glass and slammed the door.

The two men joined the women in the living room. Francisco remained by the kitchen door, unobserved by the adults yet able to hear their conversation.

"And they've doubled the size of our army," Pedro said to his brother-in-law. "Why do you think that is? To control us, of course!"

"Che Guevara — that blood-thirsty murderer — is bringing communism to a country that's not even his! Now he's forcing people to produce a certain amount each day at work or take a pay cut. He's the one behind this damn agrarian reform. Behind everything! He's a Red through and through!" Pedro slammed his fist on the chair arm.

Silvia rose from her rocker, stood by her husband, and placed her hand on his shoulder. "Pedro, it's Christmas. The children might hear you. Let me have your glass. I'll get you another daiquiri."

The living room was quiet now except for the drifting sounds of a Benny Moré record that Silvia had put on the turntable.

Francisco's thoughts turned to the mojo that Rosa had prepared to serve with the plantains. Anticipating the garlic, onion, and lime juice sauce made his mouth water. We need to have it more often, he thought. Then he remembered something his sister had said to him one evening after dinner. "Some people use food to comfort themselves, as a distraction from other thoughts. You think maybe you fit in that category?"

January 1960

$\mathcal{F}$rancisco stared at the statue as he climbed the steps of Havana University. He paused to touch an outstretched arm of the woman called Alma Mater. Bounteous mother.

"About time!" he heard his sister's voice. "Here, help me with this stuff." She shoved three heavy books toward him and picked up a large canvas bag.

"Why all this?" Francisco asked.

"It's over!" she yelled as she ran ahead of him and down the steps toward their mother's car.

Francisco tossed the books onto the back seat and slid in beside them.

"Mami, three of my professors have left — one to Tampa, one to Puerto Rico, and my sociology teacher just quit because they called him a counter-revolutionary." Luisa lowered her voice. "I heard he's going to be arrested."

"But they must have replaced them, didn't they, dear?" Silvia asked.

"Oh, sure!" Luisa nearly shouted. "With people who don't know as much as I do!" She turned toward the back seat. "Not even as much as my little brother. Mami, why? Why can't I go to Tulane?"

Silvia's voice was strained. "Now, hija, you know a girl your age can't live alone in New Orleans."

"But José and Ramón are there, Mami."

"Luisa, José is very busy in his last year of medical school. Ramón is preoccupied with his classes and his own life. We've talked about this enough. Things here will settle down. You'll have to be patient, hija."

Francisco's mother came up from behind and wrapped her arms around his shoulders. "Hijo, your father and I have a surprise. We're taking you and Luisa to the Tropicana for dinner and a show for our anniversary. Twenty-five years. That's something to celebrate, isn't it? We all need a treat and a distraction from newspaper headlines. Sound good?"

Saturday night Silvia stopped the car behind a forest-green Cadillac convertible under the curved orange roof of the Tropicana porte cochere. For a moment, Francisco felt like he was inside a pumpkin. Parking attendants swooped in to open his mother and sister's doors and a majordomo appeared to escort them to the Crystal Arches Room. As he and his father followed, he noticed for the first time how beautiful his mother looked. She wore a light-blue dress, tight around the waist and hips, its low-cut neckline showing off the diamond pendant his father had given her when Luisa was born. On their way to being seated at a table under the arches, they passed a reflecting pool where a metal ballerina twirled on a raised platform.

As he sat down, Francisco was reminded of an evening at the farm, just before dinner, when he had followed the men off the porch to a bare patch of ground. Tío Bernardo had used a stick to draw the design of the Crystal Arches and explain the concept. The nightclub walls and ceiling were made of narrow concrete arches separated by segments of curved glass. "None like it in the world," he had said. "Max Borges Jr. is the bravest architect I know."

Francisco looked at the lush vegetation inside and out, the stars clearly visible through the glass ceiling, and a stage to his right designed as a series of platforms. It was a metal geometric sculpture held together by wires with lights set into the edges of each platform.

Pedro ordered daiquiris for Silvia and him and rum and Cokes for Francisco and Luisa. Francisco took the swizzle stick from his glass and held it up. It was topped with a yellow plastic ballerina like the metal one he had seen in the reflecting pool. Soon after they arrived, dinner was served: beef filets and baked potatoes.

At 10:30, the lights along the edges of the sculpture started blinking. An announcer in a white dinner jacket and black pants stepped onto the lower stage. "Señoras y Señores of Cuba, and guests to our magical isle, the legendary Tropicana will present music heard nowhere else in the world. Spanish melodies with the cornet, piano, guitar, and bass will combine with West African drums, clave sticks, and the maracas of our own native people, and, along with a French Haitian pulse and U.S. jazz, will create a unique sound to express the spirit of the Cuban people. Lovely ladies and handsome men will dance to its rhythms."

Francisco clapped and whistled.

Twelve tall, full-figured women descended the stairs onto the first level of the stage wearing clothing that looked to Francisco like two-piece bathing suits with filmy pink material draped from their hips to their ankles. They wore purple hats with two-feet-long pink, yellow, and green feathers standing up at the front like swords.

Francisco's mother inhaled sharply and rolled her eyes. Pedro laughed, reached across the table, and squeezed his wife's hand.

Luisa leaned over. "Mami, have you seen this before?"

"Not a show like this," Silvia whispered, red-faced.

More women appeared on other stages dressed in one-piece bathing-suits with long, curved blue ostrich feathers sprouting from their hips and glittering headdresses.

Men, wearing shiny white satin shirts and tight white trousers, appeared singing and shaking their hips behind the women.

At intermission Francisco's mother took his hand. "Hijo, I didn't know it was this…"

Francisco smiled broadly. "It's great, Mami! I love the music. And everything else, too!" His father winked at him.

Following the intermission, the announcer returned to the stage. "It is an honor to present to you this evening Cuba's most famous entertainer. She sings of the beauty of this island with great love. Señoras y Señores, Celia Cruz."

The stage darkened and a single clarinet was heard. When the lower stage filled with light, a tall brown-skinned woman with an extraordinarily wide smile appeared and bowed to the audience. She wore a low-cut, gold-sequined dress that clung to her upper body and flared at her knees. Her earrings draped onto her shoulders. When she raised her arms the crowd erupted in applause and rhythmic chants of "Celia! Celia!"

The orchestra began, bringing a hush to the room until the melodic voice of Celia Cruz began singing of the joys of life. After the first song, Silvia said to everyone at the table who could hear her over the wild applause, "She's wonderful! So much better in person."

Francisco studied his mother's face. What's wonderful, he thought, is seeing you look like yourself again.

Celia sang of many things, including the beauty of her land and the love between a man and a woman. When she finished her last song, "Life is a Carnival," the previous performers returned to the stage, bowed, descended the stairs to the audience and brought the drums alive. Francisco and Luisa jumped up, pushed into the conga line of feathered women and satin-clad men, and slithered around the room. When the song finally ended, Francisco followed his sister back to the table and collapsed into his chair.

"Before we leave, Silvia," — Pedro pointed to a wide doorway, while pulling chips from his jacket pocket and rolling them in his hand — "I must go to the club room and place a bet on the wheel."

Francisco, his mother and sister followed Pedro into a room encased entirely in glass — walls and ceiling. Outside spotlights focused on tall palms that stood as sentinels above the fragile-appearing room. Francisco looked up at the stars and bumped into his father when Pedro stopped at a table covered with green felt, a roulette wheel at one end. Balanced atop the center of the wheel was a ballerina that twirled with each spin. Francisco slipped his hand between his mother and father, touching the soft felt, and then picked up some of his father's chips.

"Can I?" he asked.

Pedro shook his head. "No, son, you're too young. Move back."

February 1960

$\mathcal{F}$rancisco awoke before his alarm went off. He told himself to get up but instead turned over and closed his eyes. February first, sixteen today, he thought. Now I do have to grow up. No more goofing around. The ring his godmother had given him for his fifteenth birthday was on his bedside table. He sat up and reached for it, stroking the large lapis stone.

I was supposed to become a man at fifteen, but I didn't make it, he thought. Now I have to. Must move forward. Stop worrying about who's going to overhear what I say and report me, or who's going to be arrested. Stop being afraid of soldiers and jumping every time I see a man with a beard. I have to charge ahead and stop thinking so much. Become a lawyer and make my own life. He sat with his elbows on his knees, his chin resting in his palms. Stop being a baby, you baby.

Even though it was winter, the hallway leading to Francisco's classroom was hot. When he saw Arturo standing outside the door, he moved faster.

"Hey, man," Arturo said. "Happy birthday! You're finally catching up with the rest of us. Been a year and a half since I was young as you. What're you doing to celebrate?"

Francisco grinned, reached up, and slapped his friend on his shoulder. "We're working on that pitching arm of yours after class."

"Yeah? Not going to the club?"

"Nope. Gotta get you ready for the scouts. What happened to Connie Marrero? Did he set you up with anybody?"

Arturo whispered, "Tell you later. Mami said to tell you happy birthday." He lowered his head. "She wishes we could have you for lunch like last year, but, you know, she doesn't have her own kitchen now."

"No problem. Things will be different soon. Tell her I'll come another time."

The classroom door was open. When the boys saw Brother David step up on his platform, they slipped in, edging past desks to their own.

"Students," their teacher began in a solemn voice, "how many of you read the newspaper yesterday?"

Francisco looked around wondering how he had forgotten to read it. Three hands were raised.

Brother David walked over to the large middle window and raised it. "Can you tell your fellow classmates what it means when a government expropriates private land?"

A chill ran through Francisco. He hadn't heard the word "government," in school since the previous spring.

One of the boys who had raised his hand answered. "A government takes over land that belongs to a private person or a private company and uses it for itself or for the public."

The teacher's double white ties were now moving gently with the breeze that had entered the room. "Did this happen here recently?" he asked.

Francisco felt sweat trickling down his back.

"Yes, sir," answered the same student. "Last year the International Telephone & Telegraph Company and the Cuban Telephone Company were taken over by the government. Other companies since then."

Brother David raised his right arm and pointed his index finger toward his five rows of students, pausing in front of each before moving to the next. "Read the newspapers."

When the lunch bell rang, Francisco pushed ahead of the others and waited at the door for Arturo. He looked at the face of every person who passed. Pretty quiet today, he thought.

Arturo grabbed his sleeve. "Maybe we should go straight home after school."

"No way." Francisco shook his head. "We're getting your arm ready. Tell me what Connie Marrero said."

Arturo's smile rivaled his mother's. "It's great! I'm meeting with one of his old catchers from the Sugar Kings on Saturday. Said I could throw some for him."

"Man, great news!" Francisco punched his friend's arm. "You'll be as famous as el curvo!"

A slow, rainy weekend finally gave way to Monday morning. Francisco wove in and out among the boys in the hallway. When he stepped around the tall classmate in front of him, he saw a grinning Arturo outside their classroom door.

"You did it?" Francisco asked.

Arturo nodded. "Told me not to get my hopes up too high, but said I have promise. The Cincinnati Reds are sending a scout down in March. He'll give my name to Joe Cambria. Bet you don't know him, do you? He's the most famous scout in Cuba. Mostly works for the Washington Senators."

Francisco slapped his friend's back several times. "Wow, man. I knew you'd make it."

Arturo shook his head. "Hard to believe the first ball I ever hit was made of black tape wrapped around a cork. My bat was a limb from a guira tree. Same size from one end to the other." He exhaled loudly. "I just can't believe this, man."

The next morning Francisco sipped his café con leche while waiting for his father to slide the newspaper across the breakfast table. He needed to be prepared if Brother David asked about current-events.

A short article at the bottom of the front page described a visit from Soviet First Deputy Prime Minister Anastas Mikoyan. He had negotiated an economic agreement with Fidel to purchase five million tons of Cuban sugar over five years and agreed to supply Cuba with crude oil, wheat, iron, fertilizers, and machinery. One-hundred-million dollars in credit was extended to the Castro government.

March 5, 1960

*T*he morning newspaper headline read: "French ship, La Coubre, explodes in Havana harbor." Francisco continued reading the paragraph below: "The ship was carrying seventy-six tons of munitions purchased from Belgium intended for the army. Fidel says yesterday's destruction of La Coubre and the deaths of seventy-five to one hundred are the fault of the American CIA, says they're trying to destroy the Cuban government, says they will be made to pay."

That afternoon Francisco paced along the first-base line, watching Arturo pitch to the Belen High School hitter. It was two strikes, three balls, with two outs in the eighth inning, and he could see that his friend was tired.

"Yeah!" he shouted when the batter swung and missed Arturo's next pitch, and he jogged toward the catcher where the De La Salle team had gathered. "Great, man, you're playing like a pro." He turned to survey the crowd. "Wonder if there's a scout here?"

Arturo shook his head. "Don't know. Haven't heard anything else yet."

At home, Francisco ran past his father's open office door, realizing he had a chance to see the evening paper before dinner. Upstairs in the living room, both morning and evening papers lay neatly folded beside his father's chair. He tucked the one he wanted under his arm and quietly opened the kitchen door to see what Rosa was making for dinner. Usually she didn't like for him to bother her while she was cooking, but if she was in an especially good mood, she would give him a taste.

Rosa sat at the table smoking a cigarette and reading a small paperback book. Her hair was pulled tightly back and her face shone with a light covering of sweat in the hot kitchen. Spanish guitar music played softly on the radio. She looked up. "Hola, Panchito, you hungry already?"

"Always, Rosa." He laughed, walked to the counter, and lifted a white dishtowel covering a bowl. "Umm, a treat tonight. Your chocolate mousse." He turned and winked at her. "Is there enough for me to have a little now?"

She stood and smoothed the towel across the bowl. "If you dig into that, your mother will get us both. Now go. Dinner will be ready in half an hour."

Francisco went back to the living room and spread the newspaper on the coffee table. The first article on the front page described Fidel speaking for five hours the day before at a meeting on hotel management. He acknowledged that few tourists were coming to the island and said this was an opportunity to clean the country of undesirable elements.

He went on to decry the Eisenhower administration's attempt to harm the Cuban economy and topple the government, saying he believed the U.S. even had plans to invade the island.

Arturo was already seated at his desk when Francisco entered the classroom and waved. Arturo lay his head on his desk.

"Hey, man, what's going on? You feeling all right?"

Arturo raised his head. "Mami got a call from her aunt. Connie said the scouts aren't coming down this year. Too much going on between governments. Said I should try out for the new national teams."

"No way! Baseball, too?" Francisco leaned against his friend's desk. "But, well, what's wrong with that? They're good teams."

Arturo sat up straighter. His voice was strained. "I need to make money. They might not even pay me." He turned to face Francisco and mouthed, "And I wanted to get out of here."

"What?" Francisco lowered his voice. "You would leave your mother?"

Arturo stood and motioned for Francisco to follow him to the window. "What I wanted," he whispered, "was to play for an American team during their spring season and come back here in the winter. Remember Rudy Arias? Last year he signed with the Chicago White Sox and then played here this winter. I could see Mami then."

"Come on, man. It'll happen. They'll be here next spring."

Arturo turned to face the window. "I have to find a job. We graduate in three months. And I have to help Mami find a different place to live." He faced his friend. "You know I still sleep on the living-room couch."

Francisco lowered his head. Then he looked up and smiled. "But that makes it even more important that you work on your arm. Then you'll be ready when this ends. You gonna practice after school?"

"No," Arturo said. "I'm going to buy a lottery ticket. There's a place that's supposed to be lucky near where I used to live — close to El Encanto."

Francisco looked up at the clock on the back wall and moved toward his desk. "I'll go with you and help you choose a winner."

At lunch with his grandmother, Francisco asked her to call his mother and tell her he was getting a ride home from the club with Roberto's father so she shouldn't pick him up. He didn't like lying to his mother but felt she had become overprotective in the past few months. He was no longer free to wander around and was never allowed out after dark without an adult. He understood that the instability in the country, with soldiers on the streets and the talk of secret police, had unsettled Silvia, but he felt trapped. Yes, the atmosphere was different everywhere. People were more reserved, quieter. But hiding at home was no way to live.

Francisco and Arturo, standing in the middle of a crowded bus on the way from school to the center of Havana, swayed to "Guantanamera," a song coming from a woman's transistor radio. Francisco was enjoying himself until a dark-haired boy got on eating a Cuban sandwich — grilled pork, ham, cheese, mustard, and pickle — that made his stomach growl.

When the bus turned down Galiano Street, he pointed to the door. "Let's go. We'll walk the rest."

At the first pastry shop they passed, he grabbed his friend's arm. "Come on, I'm treating." The aroma of baked bread, sugar, and coffee filled the shop.

"Umm, that's better," Francisco murmured as he finished the last bite of his Napoleon. "Got to hurry."

The boys slowed their gait when they reached the multistory El Encanto department store.

"Man, this store always amazes me," Arturo said as he spread his arms. "Takes up a whole block. Can you believe it?" He stopped at the corner of Galiano and San Rafael streets and tapped Francisco on the shoulder. "Oye, know what this corner's called?"

Francisco shook his head, no.

"The corner of sin."

"What? Why?"

"Because people like us," he elbowed his friend, "stand here and watch really beautiful women parade in and out of that store. Can't touch, but we can look. Right?"

The boys picked up their paces to Neptuno Street, and turned the corner. Arturo pointed to a tiny store beside a beauty parlor. "Here it is. Come on." Together they decided on a lucky number and Arturo bought his ticket to a future.

"Mami, why can't I go with Roberto and his father? Carnaval is fun!"

Francisco's mother shook her head.

"But Mami. Then you and Papy take me if I can't go with them. What makes you think it's dangerous?"

His mother pointed toward the front door and mouthed, "Too many soldiers and secret police." She left the living room, went to her bedroom, and closed the door.

April 19, 1960

*F*rancisco awoke to darkness except for the dim glow of the street-lights below his window. He rolled over and pushed the alarm button on his clock radio. Its face brightened, showing 4:50. No point in getting up, he thought. Newspaper won't be here yet.

The cool breeze from the Gulf soothed him enough to allow him to fall asleep again. When he woke a second time, his room was bright. He jumped out of bed, and picked up the khaki pants he had thrown across Ramón's bed the night before and examined them. Clean enough, he thought. Mami won't notice.

His father saw him coming and pushed the paper across the table before he stood. "The communists will own us," he grumbled.

"Shipment of Soviet oil arrives today," the headline declared.

Three weeks later, another news item caught Francisco's attention: "Diplomatic relations established between Cuba and USSR."

May 1960

*B*rother David waited on the platform by his desk. The look on his face signaled quiet.

Francisco whispered to Arturo as he passed his desk, "Bought any more tickets?" Arturo shook his head.

Brother David stared over the heads of his thirty-four students toward the back wall of the classroom, and loudly cleared his throat. "Seniors, something happened last Thursday and Friday that you must be aware of. *Diario de la Marina — La Marina* — newspaper has been closed. It is said that agents working for the government took over the building and destroyed it." He went on to remind his students of its history, that *La Marina* was established in 1844 by Nicolas Rivero. His grandson, Jose Rivero, the current publisher, is now under the protection of the Peruvian Embassy.

"That newspaper had the highest circulation of any in Cuba, and a history of speaking out against corruption, wherever it existed, even in dictatorships. Many different opinions, including those of the communists, were expressed freely there. But no longer. Also on Friday, *Prensa Libre* — *Free Press* — our last newspaper independent of government control, was shut down by a mob, ending the people's right to express their opinions freely." Brother David turned toward the windows. "This is a sad day, my fellow citizens. A tragic day for our country."

Fidel's face took up the entire twelve inches of the TV screen. His words were like hammers hitting Francisco's skull: "Look at what we have accomplished in our country in the last eighteen months. We're teaching people to read, giving them health care, making a more equal society, and what do we get from Dwight David Eisenhower? More resistance to our reforms. Now he won't allow Standard Oil and Texaco to sell us gasoline or refine the oil we're buying from our friends in the USSR."

Francisco's father opened the front door. "Turn off that monstrosity! Don't believe a word he says! He's destroying this country and arresting anyone who complains."

But, Francisco thought, we were so excited when he came.

"Papy, what happened? He said he was bringing democracy. Are we certain he's lying? About everything?" His father was shaking his head. "Is it possible he's using the police just to prevent Batista supporters from taking over again while he builds houses, schools, and clinics? Aren't the poor better off now? Russia wants to help us, don't they? Does that make Fidel a communist?"

Pedro sat down on the couch and patted the cushion beside him. "Sit down, hijo. I know you want to keep your hopes up. We all wish things had turned out the way we wanted. But it's important that you accept something. Your life — our lives — won't be safe, free, happy, won't belong to us again, until this man and his government are gone. We're in danger all the time. You must not speak freely or trust anyone outside this house and family no matter how well you think you know them. And do not call attention to yourself at school or the club. Going out at night just isn't possible now for any of us. Don't make your mother repeat herself when she tells you, no."

Pedro placed his hand on his son's knee. "I'm sorry, son. You should be dating now, but we can't drive you to the parties." He faced Francisco. "Is anyone even having them?"

"A few." Francisco shook his head. "But mostly not."

"What about Marta? Are you still friendly with her?"

Francisco nodded. "I run into her at the club occasionally. She's coming with us to my class graduation party."

Pedro stood. "Good. I like her father, and her. I met him when I joined the tennis club. I've known her since she was born. Maybe later. I mean, after all this is settled, perhaps you two can go out."

Francisco's mother's face glowed as she held up the cream-colored invitation with the shield of De La Salle on the front. She opened it and pointed to his name. "*You* are reading the graduate's oath. What happened to Ricardo?"

"Remember, Mami? He's number one in the class but refused to give the baccalaureate address." Francisco threw up his hands, "Said it would make him too nervous, so Ignacio is giving it. Since I'm third, I have to do what Ignacio should have done."

Silvia jerked the chain of the living room overhead fan twice to speed it up. She pressed her palms against Francisco's cheeks. "I'm always so proud of you, hijo."

Brother David stood erect by his desk with a — by now familiar — somber look on his face. The boys stopped their chatter as they passed him and took their seats. "My sons, an announcement before I begin. U.S. diplomats have been accused by our leaders of meeting with Cuban counter-revolutionaries and have been expelled from the country." He paused long enough to focus on the faces of each of his students. "I fear for some of you and for our country. I grieve for the loss of our way of life. You are near the end of one journey while at the beginning of one unknown. I commend you for your work these past five years. You have received one of the best educations the Western Hemisphere has to offer. Your future will depend on hard work, self-discipline, and courage. As I call your names you will line up in the order of your achievement for this year."

Francisco's name was called second and Arturo's fifth. The thirty-four boys stood straight and solemn as their teacher applauded and tears streamed down his face.

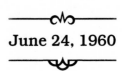

June 24, 1960

$\mathcal{F}$rancisco's mother tapped on his closed bedroom door. "Hijo, come. It's eight o'clock. We have to be there by 8:30. Graduation starts right at 9:00."

He gave his black dress shoes a last swipe with one of his brother's socks before pulling on his tuxedo jacket. As he reached in the closet for his graduation robe, he spotted his medal on the maple dresser, grinned, picked it up, and swung it over his arm.

"Mami," Francisco called as he hurried down the hall, "ready."

Silvia waited by the front door fingering her keys. She wore pearls and a straight black silk dress with lace sleeves. Diamonds set in platinum dangled from her ears. "Don't wrinkle that robe. Rosa pressed it beautifully."

She took the long, black robe from his arm, shook it gently, and brushed a hair from the shoulder of his white dinner jacket. "Hijo, don't wait to put on your eminent student medal. Do it now. I'm so proud of you. All A's — not a single

B in your five years of high school."

Francisco lifted the narrow black ribbon over his head and centered the gold medallion on his chest before smoothing down his hair.

"Now, let's go." Silvia took her son's hand. "Your father and sister will follow later in Tío Eduardo's car."

Francisco spotted Arturo's mother's head towering above the other mothers gathered with their sons in the school courtyard. Her curly bronze-tinted hair had been slicked back and gathered into a bun at the back of her head. She wore a royal blue sleeveless dress with a narrow belt at her waist.

"There they are, Mami." Francisco pointed. "Arturo and his mother."

Señora López extended her hand to them as they approached and introduced herself to Silvia by saying, "The 24th day of June, 1960. Let us hope this day marks the beginning of happy, successful lives for our sons."

"Mothers and students," the announcer barked. "Line up immediately in alphabetical order. Mothers, you will escort your son down the aisle and sit beside him during the ceremony."

Francisco's mouth was dry and his hands shook slightly as he approached the podium. He silently cursed Ricardo for putting him on a stage in front of one hundred four classmates and hundreds more aunts, uncles, siblings, parents, and grandparents. No one had given him a chance to refuse. Yet once he began reading the two-page oath, promising that the graduates would be good citizens — true to all that was good for family and country — and would be faithful Catholics, loyal to God, Francisco lost all awareness of his surroundings until he was escorting his mother down the aisle at the end of the ceremony.

"OK, hijo, I'll get the car. You find your father and Marta, and meet me at the front gate. The traffic will slow us down, so let's move along."

Francisco spotted Marta standing beside his father at the front courtyard gate.

The class party for students, their parents, and dates was held at the Havana Hilton Hotel ballroom. As Silvia followed the slow line of cars up the Hilton's circular drive, she said, "Oh, my, isn't this beautiful? Marta, dear, didn't I hear that your parents attended a reception here right after it opened?"

"Yes, Señora, I was with them. One of the architects showed us around and described it. For instance, that panel you see extending across the building above the front doors is a mosaic of Cuban fruits and flowers made with blue and white tiles from Italy. And," she hesitated, "do you want some statistics?"

"Please," Pedro said.

"The hotel has six hundred thirty rooms and thirty stories."

"Didn't know that," Francisco said. "But it does rise above everything around it."

"It's the tallest building in all of Latin America," Marta said.

The lobby, designed to look like the interior of a Spanish courtyard with plants, fountains, and statues, was filled with students and their parents. Francisco hurried through the group toward an enormous ballroom that sparkled from the tiny lights in a myriad of chandeliers hanging from the high ceiling. He spotted a table for six and waited beside it before realizing he had run ahead of Marta and his parents.

He stood on his toes, waving both arms. Marta saw him first and headed in his direction followed by his parents, Arturo, and Señora López. While Silvia introduced Arturo's mother to her husband, Francisco was struck by how much his friend had grown in recent months. He was as tall as his mother and Francisco's father. At that moment he realized he had never asked Arturo where his own father was.

A waiter in a white dinner jacket brought empanadas and fried plantains to the table. Everyone ordered a daiquiri. Soon there was the soft beating of a single drum. Heads turned toward the darkened stage. A second, then a third drum sounded before marimbas, trumpets, and flashing lights joined in.

Francisco jumped up and took Marta's hand. Arturo's mother grasped his and the dance floor was flooded with celebrants — smiling and chatting — waiting for their cue to begin the danzón.

Francisco was nervous at first but the music took over and he led Marta in the three-step slow movement, dipping and twirling her.

After dinner was served, the tres guitar, double bass, bongos, claves, maracas, piano, and trumpet awoke and *son* music filled the room. More people leapt to their feet dancing, talking, and laughing until the band left the stage at 2:00 a.m.

June 30, 1960

*P*edro slammed the front door. "It's outrageous!" he
shouted, causing Francisco to come out of the kitchen.

"What, Papy?"

"Those idiots!" He shook his head and lowered his
voice. "Now they've really done it. They nationalized three
of the biggest companies in the world — Texaco, Esso, and
Shell. The government's economic plan — if they have one
— makes no sense. We'll lose all investment from the U.S.

"Taking over businesses puts people out of work. Think
of your mother and me. The government took over the hospital and fired us, because we weren't under their thumb.
We were willing to think on our own and may have dis-
agreed with the way they ran it, but we were good at our
jobs. Did good work. And when people are out of work they
don't spend as much and boost the economy. What can they
be thinking? What are they up to?"

"But, Mami," Francisco laid his hand on his mother's forearm as she walked toward the stairs to her sisters' apartments. "We always go to the farm in the summer. Why not?"

Silvia faced her son. "I don't know what to say except we can't. We don't think it's wise right now." She turned to go and then stopped. "Hijo, too much is going on. We have your future to plan."

Francisco was both annoyed and confused. Spending two months in the summer at Guaybaque had been part of his life since he was born, and he loved it. And what did having his future to plan have to do with going to Guaybaque this summer?

Uh-oh. Suddenly he remembered that Arturo had promised to spend the first week there with them. He'd have to tell him they couldn't go. Now.

Francisco had been to the building where Arturo and his mother lived with her sister and brother-in-law only once, but since it was near the train station, that made it easier. Finally, he found the name-plate, Gonzalez Ríos, and knew he had come to the right place.

Arturo's aunt opened the door but didn't smile at Francisco or invite him in. She called for her nephew and closed the door behind him when he stepped out into the hallway. Arturo's eyes were puffy, and Francisco thought he had lost weight.

"You found out?" Arturo asked.

"What? Found out what? Did you get on a team?"

His friend lowered his head and shook it from side to side. "Mami." His voice cracked. "It's Mami." Tears came to his eyes. He stepped back, leaned against the wall and slumped to the floor.

Francisco dropped to his knees and placed his hands on his friend's shoulders. "What about her? What's wrong?"

"They arrested her!" Arturo put his head in his hands and cried softly.

"No, wait!" Francisco grabbed his friend's wrist and pulled one hand from his face. "Who? Why would anyone...?"

Arturo pushed his friend aside and stood quickly, an angry look on his face. "For counter-revolutionary statements. A neighbor told the police she heard her criticizing the government."

"They arrested her for that? That's crazy!"

Arturo stood staring at a wall, no emotion on his face.

"Where is she?"

"Don't know." Arturo sat down heavily on the floor and again wiped his face with his sleeve. "She'll have a trial but we don't know when or where. And don't even know that for certain."

Francisco lowered himself to the floor beside his friend. Twice tears pooled in his eyes but each time he felt them, he took a deep breath and shifted his attention to the water stains on the dingy hall ceiling, fearing his own show of emotion might make it harder for Arturo.

They sat quietly until a young girl ran up the stairs and stopped to look at them a moment before continuing up another flight. When they heard a door slam, Arturo leaned closer to Francisco and whispered, "My aunt told me to stay inside and not talk to anyone. I better go now."

Francisco descended the front steps of the building and kept walking straight, ending up in the middle of the street. A car swerved around him and the driver blew his horn. Stunned, he turned around to face another driver who stopped beside him and asked if he was all right. Francisco nodded yes, and stepped up onto the sidewalk.

From there he walked toward Picota Street. He noticed a church on his right but couldn't read its sign. He turned left, then right, then left again. When he realized he was beside the National Capitol Building, he walked around the entire block while looking up at its grand dome. Just like the one I saw in Washington, D.C., when I was six, he thought. We built one like theirs. And a democracy. Just like theirs.

When he got home Francisco went to his bedroom, and turned on his radio and the overhead fan. He dropped onto his bed, curled into a ball, and listened as the announcer told about the headline of the day: "U.S. passes Sugar Act, no longer giving preferential treatment to Cuban exports." The statement was followed by the playing of the Cuban national anthem. When Francisco heard the music, he instinctively jumped up, and then realized he was hungry and headed for the kitchen. Rosa was sitting at the table, a cigarette in one hand, a magazine in the other. Beaded sweat stood on her forehead despite the fan on the counter.

"Oye, Panchito. You're hungry already?" She glanced at the clock on the electric stove. "Still an hour until dinner."

"You know me, Rosa." He slumped down into the chair across from her and laid his head on the vinyl tablecloth. "But I don't think I ate lunch."

"You?" The cook laid down her magazine. "You feel all right?"

Francisco raised his head. "My friend's mother was arrested. A cleaning lady." Tears came to his eyes. "Claimed she criticized the government. Called her a counter-revolutionary."

"Shh, Panchito." Rosa stuffed her cigarette in the ashtray. "Be careful. Don't say things like that outside the house. Too many people listening." She went to the stove and lifted a towel from a bowl. "Here, I made a rice pudding for dessert. Have some now."

Dinner was unusually quick. Pedro announced that Ramón wouldn't return home for the summer but would come in time for José's wedding in September, and that José had begun his internship July first at the University of Michigan in Ann Arbor.

Silvia turned to Francisco. "Luisa is spending the night with Isabel and your father and I are going to Tío Eduardo's apartment to talk. But hijo, do not leave this house."

After his parents left, Francisco went to the kitchen. There was enough rice pudding for him to have another bowl. The kitchen was hot. He took his pudding to the living room and stood under the fan. Sweat continued to pool under his eyes. He went outside to the balcony and leaned over the railing. He pulled at the neck of his T-shirt. The only way to really cool off is to go down to the ocean, he thought. Just for a few minutes. Staying inside is giving me the creeps.

As Francisco walked the three blocks to the Malecón, the humid air was blown aside by the sea breeze. Ah, this feels great, he thought. When he reached the seawall separating the sidewalk from the water he jumped up on it, sat down, and turned around to face north. Waves lapped against the wall below him and sea gulls squawked. Somewhere in front of me, he thought, is the greatest country in the world. Our old friend. He stared at the darkness.

Where are you? What is going on between our countries? Will we go to war? No, no. He shook his head until he felt dizzy. Not possible.

Shouts and laughter to his right caused him to turn. Six young men dressed in army fatigues and carrying rifles — some slung over their shoulders and some in their hands and pointed forward — came along the sidewalk in his direction.

Telling himself to stay calm and act as if he had nothing to fear, Francisco slipped off the wall and walked stiffly across the street. Once he was a block ahead of the soldiers, he began to run.

He reached home, his heart pounding, minutes before his parents opened the door from his aunt and uncle's apartment.

"Hijo," his father said immediately. "Let's sit down in the dining room. We need to talk."

Francisco glanced at his mother's drawn face and then at his father's before taking his seat at the dining table. "What, Papy?"

"We've made a decision." His father patted the glass table. "Havana University is still in chaos. You won't get an education unless we send you to the U.S. to study. But our problem is we can't right now." He slapped the table. "Our government won't let us send our own money out of the country to pay for it!" Pedro stood, turned toward his bedroom, and called over his shoulder. "We're trying to think of a way."

Francisco's mother put her arms around Francisco. "Try not to worry, hijo."

His mind was racing. Francisco fumbled with the buttons on his shirt. Where will I go? Will I be with my brothers? Can Mami and Papy come?

July 1960

$\mathcal{F}$rancisco decided to leave his radio on, letting it play softly all day and night, in case something happened that he needed to know about. The next morning he awoke to the announcer's shrill voice: "The government of Cuba has nationalized all businesses and commercial properties belonging to citizens of the United States." Another announcement came the next evening, July sixth: "The United States has cancelled its contract to purchase seven hundred thousand tons of sugar in this year."

Francisco spent much of the next day lying on his bed under the fan or listening to the radio in the kitchen with Rosa. On the morning of July eighth, he heard that the Soviet Union would buy seven hundred thousand tons of sugar from Cuba. That evening the announcer's voice was subdued when he said that the Havana Sugar Kings were leaving Cuba. The International League baseball team, the AAA affiliate of the Cincinnati Reds, was being pulled out of its home and sent to Jersey City.

No! Francisco thought. What about Arturo?

The next morning Francisco was again awakened by the low insistent voice. This time he sat up, determined to spend the day out of the apartment and away from that voice.

Roberto was straddling a bench in the empty locker room at the club. "What's going on, man?" Francisco asked, slapping him on the shoulder.

The boy looked startled. "Just thinking," he said.

"About what?"

Roberto swung a leg over the bench and stood. He walked around the room, pushed the bathroom door open, and looked in. "OK, nobody here. Papy told me to be careful about what I say." He grinned. "He says I talk too much. We're thinking about what I'll do in September. School. What're you gonna do?"

Francisco took off his pants and pulled up his bathing suit. "Papy says I have to go to the U.S., but can't figure out how to pay for it."

Roberto sat down facing the door and whispered, "Papy heard you can send money out if — if — you study a technical career. It has to be one the government wants and our university doesn't offer, like petroleum engineering. They want that."

"Not for me." Francisco shook his head. "You know I'm going to be a lawyer."

Roberto threw up his hands. "Whatever. But don't tell anybody that. If the government finds out it's just a way for us to get out of here, they'll stop allowing it."

Francisco and Roberto joined a game of water polo in the large pool, and when it was over, they raced each other in freestyle laps until they stopped for lunch. Francisco ate his cheeseburger in four bites and gulped his chocolate milk-shake, telling Roberto he couldn't stay longer because he had something to do at home.

But instead of going home, he ran down Calzada Street toward the nearest bus stop. There he crouched in what little shade a giant bird of paradise shrub offered until the bus heading uptown stopped at the curb.

When he reached Arturo's aunt's door, he looked right, then left, wondering where the neighbor lived who had reported Señora López to the police, before knocking softly. Arturo opened the door, placed a finger across his lips, motioned for Francisco to come in, and then quietly closed it.

"Mami's still gone," he whispered. "We have to be careful of what we say, so they don't accuse her of anything else." His eyes filled with tears. "My uncle knows a man who works at the jail. He said she hasn't been sent to one of those forced-labor camps. Says she's going to trial but we don't know when."

Francisco kept his voice low. "You know the Sugar Kings are gone?"

Arturo nodded.

"What about Connie Marrero? Can he help your mom?"

"He's trying. Don't know yet."

"I heard something." Francisco leaned forward and whispered. "You can leave the country to go to school if you go into petroleum engineering. Or something like that. Something technical that Havana doesn't offer."

Arturo stepped back and turned his palms up. His voice broke. "You know I can't leave Mami."

Francisco wanted to slap Arturo on the back, tell him not to worry, his mother will be home soon, and to say something funny to distract him from his distress. But his mind was suddenly flooded with images of a single accused man sitting at a table in front of uniformed men, protesting his innocence before being dragged screaming to a wall and shot by a firing squad. He saw Che Guevara taking his gun from its holster, aiming it at the man's head as he lay wounded on the stone patio, and firing the final bullet.

Francisco exhaled. "I better go. Don't want to get you in trouble. I'll see you later."

He sat down on the curb outside Arturo's aunt's building with cars rushing by in front of him and people walking behind. He put his head in his hands, and sobbed.

Francisco lay on his bed, wet with sweat even with the fan on high. He wondered what was happening to Señora López, thinking about Arturo's comment about forced-labor camps. He assumed he was talking about the concentration camps Che had set up in the countryside for people who protested government policies, when his father opened his door.

"You went out last night," he shouted.

"Well, I . . ." Francisco stammered as he sat up. "No, Papy. Not last night."

Pedro stepped forward and raised his hand as if to strike his son. "You disobeyed me!" Terrified, Francisco bolted from the room and into the hall. His father had yelled at Ramón and had slapped his face and shoulders many times, but had never raised hand or voice to him.

Silvia peered around the corner from the dining room.

Pedro motioned to his son and his wife. "Come here, both of you. To the living room."

Luisa closed her book, and sat up on the couch. Francisco sat down beside his sister — his mind racing with questions — and his mother lowered herself into her rocker.

Pedro, his face flushed, stood in the middle of the room. His gaze was fixed on Francisco. "I received a call today from Roberto's father. Some of your friends from the club were wandering around last night. He thinks they were up to something dangerous. It's his guess that you were with them." He pointed a finger at his son. "Are you crazy? Don't you realize what's going on around you?"

Francisco raised his eyebrows and shook his head. "No. No. I don't know anything about that." He looked up at his father. "But I did go out a few nights ago. Alone." He hesitated, and then spoke hurriedly. "All I did was walk to the Malecón and sit on the wall about five minutes until I saw soldiers coming. Then I ran home." He looked at his mother. "I swear, Mami. Papy, that's all I did."

Pedro backed up and collapsed into his chair. He took several deep breaths, sighed, and wiped his cheeks with his hands.

"What happened?" Silvia asked.

"A group of boys from the club," Pedro wagged a finger at Francisco, "Roberto was one of them, were spotted roaming around. His father is afraid they'll get accused of something and get arrested. He's sending Roberto to the U.S. to study a technical career."

The four of them sat without speaking for a while.

As daylight dimmed, Pedro stood and leaned over his son. "You are getting out of this country. Forget about law school. You will be a petroleum engineer whether you like it or not."

In the morning Silvia greeted Francisco at the breakfast table and poured him a glass of orange juice. "We have work to do today, hijo, but remember, you are not allowed to leave this house. I'll call the administration office at Tulane and ask which universities offer degrees in petroleum engineering, then call them and ask for applications. Meanwhile, you will study English."

"But, Mami," Francisco said.

"Yes, I know you think you can read English, but maybe not well enough, eh, hijo? Your father is talking to Tío Eduardo about getting money from the bank."

When Rosa brought in a tray of toasted bread and café

con leche, she smiled at Francisco. "I'll make extra rice pudding today. It'll be waiting for you on the counter."

Tears came to Francisco's eyes. "Gracias, Rosa."

Out on the balcony, Francisco saw that a white haze hung across the sky between an intense blue above and an ocean so quiet it looked like a lake. Seems peaceful, he thought. But I wonder what's going on under the surface?

Francisco collected an English literature book from Luisa's room and an English grammar from his own before descending the spiral staircase to his godmother's apartment. When he walked in without knocking, she seemed a bit surprised, but smiled, laid down her needlepoint, and stretched out her arms.

"Mi Panchito, come give me a hug."

Francisco dropped briefly to her lap before settling on her sofa with the books beside him. "Madrina, I have to leave." His voice cracked. "But I don't want to. You think anyone else is going?"

"No, my boy," she said, tears in her eyes. "I'm afraid you'll be going alone. And you must go. Remember, your brothers won't be too far away."

Francisco got up and pushed the button to turn on the table fan. He stretched out on the couch. "I've never flown by myself."

His godmother picked up her needlepoint. "Sit up, Panchito. I want you to read to me. Look over there." She pointed to a bookcase behind him. "Bring that English short-story book by Eudora Welty. I like her."

A manila envelope addressed to Francisco lay on the dining-room table. He tore it open and pulled out an application to Louisiana State University in Baton Rouge, the closest school to Tulane that offered a degree in petroleum engineering. Just eighty miles from there to New Orleans, he thought. Mami says I can take a bus on Saturday mornings and spend the weekends with Ramón. He smiled. At least there was one good thing about going there.

He took the three pages downstairs to his godmother's apartment and spread them on her smooth wooden dining table. "Madrina, will you watch to see that I don't make any mistakes?"

She smiled, patted his arm, and spoke warmly, "Oh, Panchito, you won't have any trouble with this."

"It's the English," he said as he furrowed his brow.

"You read and understand it well. What are you worried about?"

He laughed and slapped his forehead. "But I can't speak a word of it!"

His godmother put her arm around his shoulders. "One step at a time, Panchito. You learn fast."

August 1960

*F*rancisco received his acceptance letter from Louisiana State University in two weeks. With the letter in hand to prove his son would be a student there, Pedro was allowed to apply to the Cuban National Bank to send money out of the country. If the Cuban government gave him permission, the bank would wire the money directly to the university, with instructions that it be used only for room, board, and tuition.

On a Monday morning in mid-August, Francisco dressed in his khaki school pants and a short-sleeved white shirt, and placed his Cuban passport and the acceptance letter from LSU in an envelope.

He found his mother folding clothes in her bedroom and leaned around the open door. "Mami, I'm ready. I'm going to get my visa."

"Wait! You know where to go, hijo?" She turned toward him. "Oh, no. Use your father's Brylcreem. Your hair's a mess."

"OK, I will. But why wouldn't I know where to go? The U.S. Embassy's two blocks from here."

Francisco walked slowly in the still, humid air. Although he was certain the embassy had air conditioning that would cool him off once he got there, he didn't want to arrive with sweat running down his face. When he turned the corner, he saw the modern, seven-story building standing prominently on Malecón Boulevard. He shook his head and moaned when he reached the front. There were two lines extending back from the tall glass front door. The line to the right held ten to twelve people, and the one on the left, twenty or more. Since they both led to a single door, Francisco was puzzled — wondering what he was missing — but he rushed to the shorter one. He looked at his watch — already 10:00, he thought. I need time to go see Arturo before Mami notices I'm not home. Thirty minutes later he reached the door. Once inside, he gave his name to a woman behind a marble counter and was directed to take a seat.

As he sought an empty chair among a grouping of forty or so straight metal ones, he saw a familiar face: Brother David, his senior class teacher. He smiled broadly at Francisco, and pointed to an empty chair beside him. "Sit, son. Tell me, where are you going?"

"Hello, Brother David. I'm going to school at Louisiana State University — petroleum engineering."

The Christian Brother chuckled. "Yes, I've heard of that option." He nodded and patted Francisco's knee. "Well, maybe someday, you'll have a chance to be a lawyer."

"What about you, sir?"

Brother David glanced around and lowered his voice.

"I'm applying for a visa to the U.S." He placed his hand on Francisco's arm, said "God be with you," and walked away.

A feeling of loss replaced Francisco's worry for his future for the next hour, until his name was called and his anxiety returned.

The consular agent shook his head and looked at the filled chairs. "Busy today," he said, and smiled before picking up Francisco's paperwork. "This looks straightforward," he murmured. "School at LSU. Awfully young, aren't you?" He paused to look at Francisco and raised his eyebrows. "Going by yourself?"

Uh-oh, Francisco thought. Do I need to tell him someone's going with me? He cleared his throat and sat up straighter. "I have two older brothers at school in the U.S. One is in New Orleans."

"Done," the agent declared as he stamped the visa and scribbled something on it before placing it in Francisco's passport. "Good for one year. Good luck to you."

Done, Francisco thought. Just like that.

He moved through the crowd, out of the cool building and onto the heat of the sidewalk. There he stopped in his tracks. Will Papy find out if I go to Arturo's? Don't know. Got to do it. He folded the envelope with his passport, visa, and acceptance letter, stuffed it in the right front pocket of his pants, and ran toward the bus stop.

There were empty seats beside the three people on the bus who were listening to transistor radios. Francisco sat down beside the one where Benny Moré was singing "Bonito y Sabroso" — Pretty and Tasty.

Francisco tapped softly on the front door of Arturo's aunt's apartment. The dark-skinned woman opened it quickly, frowning. Without speaking, she grasped his left shoulder, pulled him into the apartment, then turned down the inside hall and knocked on a door.

A wary-looking Arturo crept into the living room. His face had lost its warm chocolate color.

"I have to know," Francisco whispered.

"Let's sit down." Arturo pointed to an orange sofa covered in clear plastic.

For the first time, Francisco noticed the room. It was similar to Arturo's mother's former apartment, with bright colors on the furniture and walls and a small statue on a corner shelf, coral blossoms in a vase beside it.

"She's here," Arturo whispered as he lowered his head and covered his eyes with his hand. "She's home. They let her go with a warning."

"Man! That's good news." He wrinkled his brow. "But what did they say she did to begin with?"

Arturo smacked his right fist into his left palm. "She didn't do anything. Just complained about tourists not coming and losing her job." He lowered his voice. "Somebody doesn't like her."

Francisco lowered his voice, too. "How did she get out?"

Arturo shook his head. "My uncle thinks Connie knew somebody there."

"Now what?" Francisco asked.

"We've got to lay low. And I have to find a job." He turned away and shrugged. "Probably won't need to, though. They're sending high school graduates to teach at the new schools in the country. My guess is they'll pick me up any day now."

Francisco was hot. He looked over at the two small open windows but felt no breeze. He wanted to get up and scream at all the people in the building, the street, and the whole damn city. *What the hell is going on in my country?*

"Gotta get home. They don't know where I am," he said.

Arturo nodded.

"I'm leaving. Going to school in Louisiana. Just for a year. I'll see you next summer."

Francisco held his breath as he pulled gently on the heavy glass front door of his family's building to avoid the squeak, and slipped by his father's office. He crept up the two flights of stairs, eased open the living-room door, and tiptoed to the dining room. There he reached into his pants pocket, pulled out the envelope with his passport, visa, and acceptance letter, and laid it on the table. He went to his bedroom, changed into shorts, and lay down under the fan. He reached over and turned off his radio.

"I'm finished," he said aloud to no one. "I don't want to hear any more about revolution or arrests or people losing their jobs. No more."

At dinner Francisco's mother told him she had made his reservation to New Orleans on Delta Airlines. He was scheduled to leave September twenty-second, five days after his brother's wedding.

"But Mami, school starts before that. I'll be two weeks late!"

"I'm sorry, hijo, but you must be here for José's wedding.

And," she sighed, "flights to the U.S. are full. It was the best I could do."

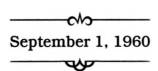

September 1, 1960

*S*ilvia, it's here. We got it!" Francisco's father called out to his wife as he slammed the living-room door and stepped into the quiet room.

Francisco was leaning back in a kitchen chair, listening to jazz on the radio and watching Rosa spoon garlic and onion sauce over sautéed chicken. He jumped up when he heard his father and went to the living room. "What, Papy? What came?"

"From the bank." Pedro waved a letter over his head. "Finally, three weeks before you leave. Those bastards finally gave me permission to send my own money to Louisiana State for your tuition," he said.

"Silvia," he called again, "where are you?"

Francisco heard the clicking of his mother's heels on the granite hall floor.

"Coming, Pedro, coming. I heard you. Now can we have his going-away dinner?" She reached up and pinched her husband's cheek. "Such a superstitious guy. Afraid

175

something might happen if we celebrate too far in advance. Our luck could backfire."

"Well, you know..." Her husband draped his arm around her shoulder. "Just needed to be sure."

Francisco's face lit up. "A party for me? Who's coming?"

Silvia bit her lower lip and smoothed her son's thick unruly hair before answering. "People are staying close to home. Not going out at night. You're very aware of that."

Francisco nodded.

"So," his mother continued, "we'll have your aunts and uncles from next door for dinner. This Saturday. And Sunday, we'll go to your grandmother's for lunch, and you'll say goodbye to her, Sofia, Clara, and Regina." She grasped his hand. "I'm sure Clara will make that orange cake you love so much." Her expression sobered. "I'm sorry, Francisco. You've worked hard and deserve a real party."

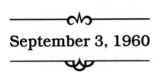

September 3, 1960

*F*rancisco's four aunts and two uncles from the three buildings beside them arrived at 8:00 p.m. Saturday. His godmother's eyes were red, as if she had been crying, but they were all dressed in their best, smiling and congratulating him on his acceptance to LSU.

Tío Bernardo pulled Francisco aside and said, "I want to show you something. Let's go to your room."

Francisco picked up the shorts he had left on the floor when he was getting dressed for dinner. "Sorry, Tío, I'm a slob."

His uncle grinned. "Me, too." He waved his hand. "Don't bother with that, Panchito. I've something I want you to see." He took a long slender black box from his guayabera shirt pocket and held it out to Francisco. "This is for you."

"What is it?" he asked as he opened the box.

Bernardo lifted the pen from his nephew's hands and held it up. "This is the pen I used to trace the final plans for the design of the Maine Monument." His gentle gaze rested on Francisco. "I want you to have it."

Francisco's eyes widened, and his mouth fell open. "Me?" Francisco was surprised. Although he was fascinated by his uncle's creativity, proud of his accomplishments, and loved his wild stories, he didn't feel especially close to him. "Why me?" he blurted out. "I mean," he hesitated, "thank you. I won't lose it. I promise."

Bernardo hugged him and chuckled. "I know you won't. Be sure to take it with you and use it. I like knowing it'll be in the U.S."

Francisco passed Tío Eduardo on his way back to the living room. His uncle grasped his left shoulder and stuffed something in the right back pocket of his pants. "Hang onto that, boy," he said. "You'll need it."

Francisco returned to his room, slipped three fingers in his pocket and pulled out five twenty-dollar bills.

Silvia and Elena were spreading a white lace tablecloth across the dining table and the smaller table they had set up at the end when Francisco returned to the dining room.

"Hijo," his mother said as she pointed to a chair at the middle of the table. "You sit there."

Francisco grinned as Rosa placed a heaping bowl of zarzuela de mariscos on the table in front of him before returning with a bowl of arroz amarillo and a platter of ensalada de aguacate. His mouth watered as he spooned the lobster and crab-filled stew over his rice and heaped a large spoonful of avocado salad beside it.

The men were seated at the end of the table to Francisco's left and the women were to his right. Luisa sat across from

him. The room was filled with laughter and shouts as each
of the three men tried to assert his opinion and drown out
the others. The women gave up trying to be involved in
their conversation, turned to each other, and chatted about
children and friends from the club. His sister was quiet, appearing as surprised as he at the boisterous adults.

Francisco tried to remember the last time he experi-
enced what, in the past, had been commonplace at his dinner table. At the farm last summer, he thought. Well, no,
not even then, but maybe a year and a half ago. It felt good
seeing the people he loved happy. Then he asked himself:
will I see it again?

After everyone finished the orange cake and espresso
the men stepped out on the balcony and closed the sliding
glass door behind them. Francisco watched as they lit cigars
and leaned forward into their now-familiar huddle. There
they go again, he thought. The women retreated to his godmother's apartment and Luisa to her bedroom. He turned
on the television for a few minutes, then turned it off and
went to his room, wondering why a perfect evening had to
end this way.

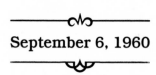

September 6, 1960

*J*ust what we need," Pedro said, placing an emphasis on each word.

Francisco's mother stood for a moment and stared at her husband before taking her seat at the dinner table. "What, dear?"

"What *now*, would be a better way to ask it, Silvia."

Rosa stopped at the kitchen door. Luisa laid her book beside her plate. Francisco sat up straight.

"We've got a real hurricane coming toward us. A patient just told me it's supposed to reach The Bahamas tomorrow, then probably head here."

"Oh, no." Silvia looked at Rosa. "Let's see if we have enough candles."

"Are they sure?" Francisco asked.

"Never know for certain. The Americans named it Donna, and say it's already a Category 3. She's a big one." He picked up his fork and knife. "Of course, we've been living through Category 4 destruction for a year and a half," he chuckled. "Guess we can handle a little wind and water."

Francisco turned his radio back on that evening when he went to bed.

The next morning Francisco looked out his window toward the Gulf. The blue sky was filled with a few large white clouds, but the water was calm.

Later in the day the radio announcer described thirteen-foot water surges and one-hundred-fifty-mile-an-hour winds lashing The Bahamas: "On its way! Headed straight for Cuba!" He sounded the same as when he described Fidel's journey from the mountains to Havana, Francisco thought.

September 10, 1960

*S*aturday morning the radio announcer spoke quickly, "The northeastern coast of Cuba is scraped and bleeding, but Havana is spared. Donna is turning north for Florida Keys and the U.S. mainland."

Francisco shivered. No bullet for us this time, he thought. He grabbed his bathing suit, wrote his mother a note telling her where he would be and left for the club.

Two boys were in the locker room — one called Colorado because he blushed every time he was spoken to, and a friend of his from the yacht club whom Francisco didn't know.

Francisco spotted his sister lying by the pool on a lounge chair, a book in her hand. "What are you doing here?" he asked.

Luisa didn't take her eyes off the book. "Why wouldn't I be?"

"I thought you'd be at the Biltmore with Isabel."

"She's gone."

"Gone? Where?"

Luisa swung her legs over the side of the chair and sat up, facing her brother. "You can't ask that question. Just gone." She hesitated and lowered her voice. "The people you're looking for are at the handball court."

"How do you know...? OK, thanks."

Francisco pushed on the heavy double doors leading to the court. He heard sneakers slapping the wooden floor and muted voices, but saw no one. He went behind the left wall to a supply closet. "Hey, anybody in there?" he called. The door bumped his nose as it was flung open. Four boys came out of the closet — two he had seen around but didn't know well. Another was a guy from his class named Eugenio who was cradling a stack of printed sheets of paper in his arms. The fourth was Roberto.

"What's going on?" Francisco turned to Roberto.

Roberto turned away and shook his head. Eugenio stuffed the papers into a small green duffle bag and nodded. "Gotta go. See you later."

Roberto grabbed Francisco's arm. "Come on. Let's play basketball."

September 13, 1960

*I*t was an especially hot evening so Silvia had turned on
the overhead fan and opened the balcony door. Francisco
was listening to the music that drifted up from the neighbor
below. He, his mother, father, and sister were finishing dinner. The ringing of the outside doorbell downstairs caused
him to jump. He twisted his wrist to look at his watch, causing his last bite of black beans and rice to fall off his fork.

"Somebody pushing the wrong bell," his father said.
"They'll figure it out."

When the ringing continued, Pedro slapped his napkin
on the table and went downstairs. "No, no!" His voice rose
until Francisco could hear it. "What do you want with him?
Go away!"

Francisco ran down the two flights of stairs, nearly trip-
ping on the first landing, but stayed ahead of his mother and
sister.

"Papy, what?"

Two young men with thin beards, dressed in military

fatigues, stood outside. Guns in holsters dangled from their belts. "Our orders are to take Francisco Pérez Soler to the police station."

"No!" Pedro said. "What police station?"

The taller soldier pointed left. "Two blocks that way."

"But why?" Francisco asked. He stepped in front of his father.

Silvia grabbed her son's arm, and pulled him toward her.

The shorter man spoke. "Captain García sent for you."

The other patted his holster. "You have no choice."

Pedro backed into the glass door causing Silvia to cry out. "All right, I'll take him," he said. "We'll walk over."

"No," the taller man spoke. "You're not allowed. He has to go with us in the car." He pointed to a small brown vehicle.

Many thoughts flitted through Francisco's mind at that moment, but only two made themselves clear: puzzlement, and fear for his father. He needed to find out what the police wanted of him and to remove these soldiers from his home before someone did something rash. He pulled away from his mother. "Here I am. I'll go."

Luisa wrapped her arms around her mother, who was now screaming and crying.

Pedro grasped his son's shoulders and looked in his eyes. "I'll make some calls. Then I'll be there. Waiting outside."

An older gray-haired soldier sat behind the reception desk in the police station. He pointed to a group of ten boys huddled together in a corner of the brightly-lit room. Roberto and Eugenio were among them.

A door opened. Captain García entered carrying a single sheet of paper, and said, "Follow me."

He knows us from the club, Francisco thought. He knows Papy. It'll be OK. He stepped in front of another boy and tried to make eye contact with the captain, but he turned away.

Captain García ushered the eleven boys to an empty room and closed the door. He pointed to the middle of the floor. "Sit."

They sat down close together where the captain had pointed. He stood for a few minutes and stared at them. "Some of you here, maybe all of you, have been passing this." He held up the printed sheet of paper. "Anti-government and counter-revolutionary. What can you be thinking?" His face reddened as he shouted, "You are stupid!" Then his voice fell. "You don't know what you're getting into."

Slowly the captain walked around the boys, then stood before them again and smiled. He pointed to the few gray hairs on his temples. "Believe it or not, I was young once — even as young as you."

Then he stopped smiling and took a step back. "But I'm sure I was smarter. If this happens again G2 will get involved. You know, the secret police? They're not like me. They mean business." He shook his head. "No, trust me. You don't want that to happen."

Captain García looked at each of them in turn. "Let me tell you what they'll do. First, they'll put you in a small, dark room — alone. Then they'll pull in some of your friends. Throw them in jail for two or three months, and then see what they have to say about you. And I assure you, it won't matter who your father knows. There will be nothing anyone can do to help you."

No sound or movement came from the group. Francisco held his breath. Sweat ran down his sides. He looked up at the captain. There was nothing familiar about the man in front of him. Is this the man I know? he asked himself.

"Boys," the captain said, "if you have any of these, burn them." He held up the printed sheet. "And go stay with somebody outside Havana. Disappear. Don't show your faces. Just leave for a while!"

Francisco felt as if he had been kicked in the gut. He concentrated on making himself invisible by lowering his head, clasping his sweaty hands to his lap, and breathing shallowly while he waited in the reception room for the two soldiers who had brought him to the police station to drive him home. He looked around outside the station for his father, but he wasn't there.

As he leapt up the stairs two-at-a-time, he gasped when he saw the living room door ajar. They don't ever leave that door open. Where are they? he wondered.

His mother appeared and ran toward him. "I've been listening for you." Her face was pale and her eyes were red. Once in the living room, she pulled him down beside her on the couch and leaned against him. "Are you OK? Did they hurt you?"

Pedro was on the phone. "We have to change that ticket, Teresa. Tonight, tomorrow, as soon as you can. Yes, I know it'll cost extra. Just get him a seat." He hung up the phone and turned to his son, his voice breaking. "You're going to Louisiana, son. Get ready. Teresa, my friend's niece, works for Delta. She'll get you out." Then he grasped Francisco's hand. "I've been on the phone since they took you. I'm sorry I couldn't be there." Pedro stood straighter. "Now, go. Pack."

Silvia stood. "Take all your clothes and everything that's important to you. But," she frowned, "you're only allowed one suitcase."

"Mami, it's just for nine months. I'll be back in June. Or Christmas. Won't I be coming home for...?" Francisco started down the hall, and then turned. "What about José's wedding? I won't be here, will I?"

Pedro interrupted. "Do what your mother told you. Now!"

September 15, 1960

*F*rancisco awoke at 6:00 before his alarm rang. He had slept about thirty minutes just before dawn. He went to the window overlooking Calzada Street, leaned against the sill, and stared at the calm waters of the bay. The sky was a soft golden color — no dark clouds above the horizon. Maybe my flight *will* make it to New Orleans.

He crept out of his room and down the hall to the kitchen. Rosa hadn't come out of her room, but his mother and father sat at the table sipping coffee. Their faces were somber — his mother's was a blotchy-red and his father's was pale blue. Silvia stood and gave him a long hug. Then she made café con leche for him, poured orange juice, and dropped two pieces of bread into the toaster. She turned to him. "Hijo, are you...?" Her voice broke and she wiped tears from her cheeks.

At 11:00 a.m. Francisco shoved his suitcase into the Chrysler's trunk and slid into the back seat beside Luisa.

His father sat in the front passenger seat beside his mother who was watching in the rearview mirror while Tío Eduardo pulled in behind them. Tía Julia was beside her husband in the front seat of the Ford Fairlane, and Francisco's godmother and Tía Tita were the backseat.

The Rancho Boyeros airport was a two-story tan stucco building with a tower in the center. Silvia and Eduardo parked their cars in front. No one spoke as they filed pass the Pan American and Cubana airlines desks on their way to Delta. Francisco and his father stood in line there, allowing others to pass, until Teresa was available to check Francisco in.

Francisco followed his family to the visitors' waiting room. It was a long hall, with chairs on one side and glass panels on the other. The glass separated this room from the passenger waiting room but allowed the people in both areas to see each other. After the last of the hugs and goodbyes, he opened the door to the passengers' room. It held fifty or so red molded-plastic chairs and a large clock on the left wall that showed hours, minutes, and seconds. Although nearly every chair was filled, Francisco found one that faced his family. He waved and smiled. His mother and aunts waved back. His godmother pulled a camera from her purse, held it against the glass, and snapped. He watched as Tío Eduardo reached for a cigarette and placed it in his mouth only to discover another one there. They sat without talking and stared at him. His only feeling was of mental and physical exhaustion.

When beads of sweat began rolling down his sides, Francisco looked up. No fan. His mother had insisted that he wear two shirts because he would be sleeping on a couch that night in New Orleans, and she thought he might be cold. The plan was for Juan, José's fiancée's brother, to pick him up at the airport and take him to his apartment to spend the night. At 3:00 a.m. the next morning they would leave for Louisiana State where Juan would drop him off and make it back to Tulane in time for his 2:00 p.m. class. Francisco noticed that most of the people in the room were doing the same things he was — fanning themselves, and looking from their watches to the clock. A few were pacing around the room. No one was talking. He checked the time again — twenty-four minutes before Delta Flight 30 was scheduled to depart.

Francisco was wondering where the single door on the wall to his right led when it opened and a man in his twenties with a thick beard and dressed in a military uniform emerged and called out, "Francisco Pedro Pérez Soler."

Was that my name? he asked himself. No, no, couldn't be. When the military man stepped farther into the waiting room, Francisco noticed he had a limp.

Again he called, "Francisco Pedro Pérez Soler."

Francisco jumped up and raised his hand. "Me. Yes. I'm here." As he stood, he glanced at his family. His father and uncle were on their feet. His mother and sister had covered their mouths with their hands. Tía Julia leaned against his godmother.

As Francisco approached, the young man turned toward the open door and motioned for him to follow.

The room Francisco entered was lit with two rows of long fluorescent bulbs hanging from chains, positioned directly above a narrow table in the center. Three wooden chairs stood on one side of the table and one other on the other side facing them. A window to the tarmac was on one wall but no glass panels joined this room and the waiting room. Francisco looked out and saw suitcases being loaded into the luggage compartment of the Delta DC-7.

Two more men — another in his twenties and one in his forties — bearded and dressed the same as the first, sat at the table. They wore diamond insignias — half red and half black with twenty-six in the middle — on their shirt-sleeves. The older man removed his hat and told Francisco to sit down.

Francisco felt dizzy. He held onto the back of the chair for a moment before sitting. "What's wrong?" he asked.

The men looked at each other and chuckled. The young one without the limp slapped his hat on the table and growled, "We're asking you the questions."

Then question after question was fired at Francisco. "Why are you leaving our beautiful fatherland? What will you study? Where? Why can't you do that here? When will you return? Where do you live? What do your father and mother do? What about your siblings? Why are your brothers out of the country?"

Relax, relax, Francisco kept telling himself. Don't look guilty. He tried to stop his hands and jaw from shaking by resting his chin in his hands while he answered the questions as thoroughly as possible. Once tears surfaced, but he worked to keep them to himself, along with his own question — why are you doing this to me?

"What do you and your family think of the revolution?" a young soldier asked, leaning forward in his chair.

Francisco took a deep breath and raised his fist. "We're proud of our country!"

The soldiers paused and whispered something to each other. Francisco turned to the window: The last person in line was climbing the steps of the plane.

The older soldier then asked, "Where did this name of yours — Soler — come from? Is it Cuban?"

And from the young man with the limp, "Are you related to Carlos Soler?"

With that question, Francisco was stuck. He had no good answers. His mother's brother, Carlos, was an unusual man. He had written letters of support to Batista when he was in power — though most people opposed him — and contradictory letters supporting revolution. As a physician, his shabby office was located in the poorer section of Havana. He performed abortions in this Catholic country where they were illegal and considered immoral.

And Carlos experimented with medical procedures that were sometimes not likely to succeed. Francisco wondered what this man blamed him for and knew it was safer to deny any connection with him. On the other hand, the only people in Cuba named Soler were his mother's large family, so there was no escaping his relationship to Tío Carlos. He was afraid to lie. Either way, he knew it was likely that he would be taken from this room and disappear for years.

He sighed and, his voice breaking, said, "Yes, Carlos Soler is my uncle."

The face of the young man with the limp lit up. He grinned, smacked the table, and turned to his comrades.

"That doctor saved my mother's life when no one else could help her. He's a great man!"

The three men shoved their chairs back and stood. "Get up. Out of here." The older soldier pointed a thumb toward the door. "We're done."

Francisco stumbled toward the waiting room door. When he opened it, he saw all his relatives leaning against the glass panels. Everyone except Tío Eduardo was crying. He waved both arms and blew kisses to them. Tears slipped down his cheeks. Then he turned away, ran past the desk, and out to the tarmac. The door of the plane was still open.

Shortly after Delta Flight 30 rose to the sky, the pilot announced, "Señoras y Señores, we are now over glorious, shimmering, free international waters." The passengers clapped and roared.

Epilogue

*T*he Cuban government permitted its citizens to leave the country directly for the United States until diplomatic relations were severed between the two countries on January 3, 1961. They were allowed to take one suitcase per person, but no valuables and only enough money for a short visit. If they stayed away for longer than thirty days, all their personal property was taken by the state.

At the end of Francisco's first year at Louisiana State University, he traveled to Ann Arbor, Michigan, to spend the summer with his family. While there, he applied for a transfer to the University of Michigan and was accepted, able to afford the tuition only because the university awarded him in-state status. While in school, he worked at various jobs before settling into working with mice in the university allergy lab. After finishing medical school at age twenty-three, he remained at Michigan to complete a residency in radiology. Drafted during the Vietnam War, he spent two years with the United States Air Force in Texas. After his service, he practiced radiology for thirty-five years before retiring.

Luisa enrolled for the 1960 fall semester at the University of Havana. In October, she was picked up by the police while selling the student newspaper on campus. Unknown to her, that very day the military had closed it down and arrested its editor. A friend from high school who had joined the communists pulled her out of the group surrounding her, drove her home, and told her parents she must leave the country or she would be arrested.

She was on a plane bound for Michigan two days later, October 22, 1960, where she moved in with her brother, José and her sister-in-law. She found work as a secretary, and in September 1961 enrolled at the University of Michigan, continuing to work part-time until finishing a master's degree in social work.

Pedro applied for permission from the Cuban government to attend an International Conference in Orthopedics in July 1961. He and Silvia were allowed to take enough money to cover their expenses for one week. Once in Michigan, they moved in with José, his wife, and Luisa. Although she had never sewn in her life, Silvia immediately found a job repairing clothing at a dry cleaner's shop. Pedro began work in the bone bank at the university.

Ramón worked part-time to pay his tuition for his last year at Tulane. He graduated with a degree in architecture and began his career with a private architectural firm in New Orleans.

José completed an orthopedics residency at the University of Michigan. He served his chosen field in both academic medicine and private practice until retirement.

Grandmother Twenty-one, and her sister, Sofia, along with Aunts Clara, Elena, Tita, and Uncle Eduardo, left Cuba in 1969 under the pretense of vacationing in Mexico. Luisa met them there to help obtain a Mexican visa, thereby allowing them to remain in that country while they applied for a visa to travel to the United States. The family exhausted their savings and borrowed the remainder of the many thousands of dollars required to purchase the Mexican visa. Eduardo's brother in Miami contributed and continued to subsidize him until his death. José petitioned Hale Boggs, a member of the U.S. House of Representatives from Louisiana, for help in obtaining a green card that granted them permanent residency in the United States.

Aunts Julia and Regina had died of breast cancer in Cuba — Julia in 1964, and Regina in 1967.

Uncle Carlos and his family left Cuba for Miami in late summer, 1960. His children graduated from college, becoming architects and other professionals. One of his adult sons remained in Cuba and lived on the farm until he was killed in a traffic accident in 1965.

Uncle Bernardo and Aunt Raquel never left Cuba. The eagle sculpture that he designed for the top of the Maine Monument was pulled down and smashed into pieces by an anti-American mob in 1961. The eagle's head was given to the Swiss government, the caretakers of the former United States Embassy building. At the re-opening of the embassy in August 2015, it was hung in the entrance hall. Other parts of the sculpture were given to a history museum in Havana.

Cousins Tomás Cuervo and Anna left for Miami in July 1960. Anna opened a catering business there. Tomás' assistant, Manny, went with them.

Arturo was sent by the government to the countryside to teach school for two years before being encouraged to join the Cuban National Baseball Team. Because all members were required to join the Communist Party, he refused. He was approached many times, and each time declined. Finally, he was sent to harvest sugarcane and died at age fifty-two. Señora López continued to live with her sister until she disappeared in 1970.

Rosa moved in with her brother and his family in Santiago de Cuba and found part-time work as a dishwasher.

Roberto's family left Cuba in the fall of 1960 for Tampa, Florida, where his father's family owned a restaurant and bakery. In September 1961, he enrolled at Louisiana State University. The blue and white Mercury convertible, as well as all the other possessions his father so loved were taken by the government.

The Christian Brothers were harassed and arrested, some sent to La Cabaña prison and others to work camps. In the fall of 1960, Francisco's sophomore-year teacher, Brother Cepillo, was fatally shot on the sidewalk in front of De La Salle while trying to prevent soldiers from entering the school.

One hundred of the one hundred five students graduating with Francisco's high school class in 1960 fled the country. De La Salle School was closed May 1, 1961, when the Cuban government nationalized all private schools and confiscated their properties. On May 25, 1961, all Christian

Brothers, priests, and nuns, were expelled from the country.

Francisco's family's farm, Guaybaque, was taken by the government after Uncle Carlos' son was killed. It was used as a place for rest and relaxation by members of the military. Humberto asked for a parcel for his family as part of the land redistribution program, but was denied. He moved into an apartment in Matanzas. Uncle Bernardo's castle was given to a relative of the head of the Communist Party. Fidel Castro's sister moved into one of the other houses on the property.

Many wealthy and famous people left the island, too. Celia Cruz moved to Mexico and then on to the United States, where she died in New Jersey in 2003. Ernest Hemingway abandoned his beloved home outside of Havana, Finca Vigia, on July 25, 1960.

April 17, 1961

Fourteen hundred Cuban counter-revolutionary exiles, trained and financed by the American Central Intelligence Agency, launched an attack at the Bay of Pigs in southern Cuba. The promise of U.S. naval and air back-up never materialized, and they were defeated in two days by a much larger Cuban military force. Francisco attempted to sign up for this expedition but was rejected because he was not yet eighteen years-old.

October 1962

The Soviet Union placed medium-range ballistic nuclear missiles in Cuba, directed toward the United States to deter another U.S. government-sponsored attempt to invade the island. In response, U.S. President John F. Kennedy imposed a quarantine encircling Cuba to prevent any Soviet ship containing nuclear components from landing on the island. He informed the Kremlin that the U.S. would launch a nuclear attack against the Soviet Union if it attacked the U.S.

Premier Nikita Khrushchev and President Kennedy negotiated directly to remove the Soviet missiles, on the condition that the United States would not invade the island and would remove its own missiles from Turkey. The U.S. government then set up an official trade embargo on Cuba and banned American citizens from traveling directly to the island and spending money there.

February 24, 2008

$\mathcal{F}$idel Castro held complete power over the whole of Cuban society — its public and private life — as a totalitarian dictator for forty-nine years before handing the reins permanently to his brother, Raúl. In an attempt to rescue his failed economy, Raúl Castro loosened restrictions on his citizens somewhat by allowing them to buy and sell private property and receive an exit visa more easily.

However, as of February 2016, the police state against the Cuban people by Raúl Castro continued unmitigated.

Acknowledgements

$\mathcal{J}$did not write this book alone. Each person who cared enough to become involved provided me with a leg up. My husband spent many hours describing the first sixteen years of his life in Cuba. Doing so brought forth happy memories but also painful feelings of helplessness and loss. Friends, Kathy and Gary Bovard, offered a crucial idea for the beginning of the story. And many thanks to editors Nora Gaskin Esthimer and Linda W. Hobson. Together we made it happen.

–Linda Hardister Rodriguez

Also by Linda Hardister Rodriguez...

IMAGINE. You're a small town southern factory worker—disabled on the job—and you believe what your boss, your surgeon, and the government bureaucracy tell you. Everything will be fine. All you have to do is wait. You will return to your middle class life. Imagine people lying to you.

As Matt Bradfurd is swept into poverty, he struggles with the belief that a man should make it on his own. When he's in danger of losing his home and his wife and daughter are hungry, he overcomes his pride and reaches out to three community leaders. Their response creates a story of greed and betrayal making us question what's important in life.